Blood Relation

Marie Valden

Artwork: Cristen L. Canole

Dragonfly Press

Dallas, Texas
Dragonflypresss.org

ISBN 978-0-9989405-9-5

Dedication

To A, B, C, D, my 4 halos, for without you I would have no words.

This story is dedicated to all those who have lived through, fought to get out of and survived the dysfunction of familial trauma.

Chapter One

"No!" Rose broke into heaving sobs as her thin, trembling body slid down the door. She sat on her heels, both fists at the ready. Unable to gauge her surroundings, she collapsed in a heap on the floor. A man's voice called out her name gentle hands lifted her off the floor.

A cup of hot tea materialized in front of her. Whispered voices came from behind. Then a familiar face appeared before her.

"Rose," the man shook his head then produced a slight grin, "don't be discouraged."

He wore a white coat. *A doctor?* She looked at the name embroidered on his pocket.

"Dr. Grant?"

"Do you know where you are?"

"Back in your office?" Her voice cracked.

"Good, you're waking up now. You'll be back to normal shortly." He patted her on the shoulder as he gingerly guided her to the wingback chair she had bolted out of. "When you explode out of your hypnotic state like that it takes a few extra minutes to adjust. With repeated efforts, repressed memories will surface. That's why, I'm certain, with a few days at Baylor-"

"A few days at Baylor, are you nuts!" She blurted. "I've spent the last ten years in your office trying to get to the bottom of why I can't sleep at night. I agreed to the hypnotherapy stuff. But the hospital is out." She put the cup of tea down on the side table of the chair, hard.

Dr. Grant cleared his throat, "As I was saying, if we get to the truth, I believe all of your symptoms will vanish."

Rose stood, abruptly rubbing her sweaty palms against her black skinny jeans. "You've said that before. I'm not going to keep doing this. I have a ton of press junkets coming up for *Midnight.* Chapter revisions I still haven't been able to finish. And, if that's not enough, I have a book signing in Atlanta day after tomorrow. Atlanta!" Rose paced, "If the press got wind of this . . ." She collapsed back into the chair. "No. Can't you just give me something to make it all go away?"

"You are so close to the truth but your fears are stopping you from remembering. I wish there was a pill but there isn't. It just takes picking away at it until something breaks."

"You mean my sanity. So, how am I gonna get through the next few days?"

"If we had your biological family's physical and mental health-history we could rule out a psychosis." Dr. Grant removed his glasses and lifted one eyebrow, "While you're in Atlanta, it would be beneficial to get your birth parents' medical history. I'll give you a prescription for Xanax so you can sleep but that's the best I can do until you're ready to face your demons." He rose silently and made his way to the desk.

The cabinet clock struck on the hour. Looking around the office, Rose could see why she was so at-home. There were seating areas compartmentalized throughout the huge book case lined office. Several Persian style rugs and heavy damask draperies kept the noise to a minimum. Deep, rich colors and dark cherrywood served as a back drop for the art and beautiful crystal collection of antique medical jars and bottles he kept on display to the right of his huge Mahogany desk with lion claw legs. She reflected how well he fit behind that desk. He wasn't a white-washed pale skinned, balding doctor. He was trim and fit with a full head of chestnut-colored curls and a well-earned tan. His eyes soft and inviting had always captivated her during their sessions. His voice shook her into the present.

"That's it for today," he said, as he tore a sheet from his prescription pad. "Give the hospital some consideration and when you get back in town call me." He glanced at the script and then handed it to Rose. "I believe you can work through this we just need to find the key to open the box you've locked your childhood boogeyman in." He spoke softly and reassuringly as he walked her to the door. She did not like feeling patronized.

Exiting the building the night breeze hit her face with a refreshingly, bitter coldness. An all too familiar sense that she wasn't alone sent a chill up her spine as the hair on her arms prickled. She settled into the customized black Alpha Romero with tinted windows and a convertible top. She loved driving with the top down underneath the stars. The night sky blanketed her heart with the promise of protection that made her feel safe. Seeing a shrink at night had its advantages too, free curbside parking.

⋅⋅⧫⧫⧫⋅⋅

Rose startled awake in her first-class seat on the red eye to Atlanta struggling to look not embarrassed. She used her last sip of cabernet to wash down the terror her dreams always left her with. She couldn't grasp the dream fully. It was always a distant taunt, hiding behind the dark curtain that shrouded the deepest recesses of her mind. The plane to Atlanta was thankfully sparse of passengers and it appeared that no one had witnessed her sharp awakening.

"Ma'am?"

Rose flinched in response to the voice of the flight attendant lurking just behind her seat.

The pretty blonde attendant hovered. "Are you alright? Can I get you something?"

After she returned with another wine Rose agreed, "Of course, I'll be glad to autograph your book."

"My mother loves your books. Constantine is the best vampire ever. He's mean and nasty and oh, so romantic. I'd let him bite me." The attendant smiled wide as she walked away with her prized autographed vampire book.

Rose laid her head back took several deep cleansing breaths and started to relax again. She heard a distant, raggedy breath but there was no one in the seat beside her, it had to be someone in a seat behind her, right? She chose to ignore it and allowed her body to relax even deeper. The gentle roar of the plane helped to lull her. Her skin chilled and then prickled. The ding from the "fasten your seat belt" sign echoed from far away. A slight dip in pressure let her know they were descending, when she felt a breath of cold air on her neck. Her arm wanted to reach for the offensive breeze but it failed to flinch. *I must be dreaming.* A colder sharp thing lapped at her neck. A voice deep and resonate whispered. "Welcome home Rose." *A man's voice!*

Rose jerked in her seat her arms flailed at air. Still, no one sat next to her. The nearest person was two rows over and they were wearing an eye mask. The plane echoed with stillness once again. Chills clawed their way up her spine, the distant laughter of a child echoed. She rang for the flight attendant.

"Ms. Bodin, How can I help you?"

"Are we on schedule?"

"Yes Ma'am, we'll be in Atlanta in about thirty-five minutes, barring traffic." She made a circling motion with her finger in the air, "can I get you anything?"

"No, thanks."

Rose put away her laptop as the Captain announced their final approach to the Atlanta Hartsfeld-Jackson International airport. The words grabbed her throat. She took one last gulp of her wine to clear the lump. *Ahhh! First class!*

Rose took quick steps on the moving sidewalk that gave her a good head start from the spattering of passengers aimed for the baggage claim. At the top of the escalator a young man held a sign with her code name in large letters, VELMA. Jeff, her publicist, had recommended it after she had been bombarded by fans at LAX two years ago. She chose the name from her favorite cartoon, Scooby Doo. Television was a great escape for a girl who couldn't go outside to play. Books became Rose's best friend. It's easier now with computers and texting, she never has to leave the safety of her condo except for book signings.

The buff young man at the top of the escalators had the appearance of an athlete. Strawberry blonde locks he pushed off of his forehead at regular intervals and the light freckling across the bridge of his nose gave him a boyish look. The big toothy grin didn't help. But, attached to his well-tailored suit lapel was a single red rose bud. She smiled at the thought that he might have worn it to impress her. Behind him an airport cart, complete with driver, sat at the ready. The young man stepped to one side and took a deep bow, "Ms. Bodin, allow me to introduce myself, I am Jeremy James Hayden, the third, at your service."

"Thank you, Jeremy."

"It's a pleasure, Ma'am."

Rose extended her hand. "Call me Rose."

"It's an honor. I was instructed to tell you that your publicist, Jeff, hired me to escort you to your hotel and tend to whatever you may need. Your chariot, Ma'am."

Jeff thinks of everything. "Thank you, Jeremy, but lay off the Ma'am stuff I'm not that old, yet." Rose waved her hand across her neck as to say, cut it off.

"Yes, Rose." Jeremy smiled so hard his ears lifted with a tinge of red on the tips.

They boarded the cart moments before the other passengers reached the top of the escalators. Not ready to face a crowd she had no control over, Rose sighed with relief to finally be on her way.

Once safe in the limousine Rose reclined deep into the leather bench seat, engaged the down button for the window. Early birds chirped as they greeted the night surrendering sky while it ushered in the faintest glimmer of dawn pregnant on the distant horizon. The aromas of spring filled the car with a sweetness. The wheels of the limo hummed beneath her with a false serenity. Grand mansions along oak lined avenues gave way to modern skyscrapers and strip malls. The city emitted a rhythm like nowhere else she'd been. It called to her. She smiled. She'd timed it just right. The sun wouldn't be a threat to her until after she reached the safety of the hotel. The pungent, sweet, smell of Magnolia grabbed the back of her throat and caused a violent gag. She knew it was Magnolia. Once, at the age of 7, she fainted after smelling a blossom on the tree. She spent three days in Children's Hospital with, what doctors later called, a self-induced coma. No one could explain but speculated the tree had something to do with an allergy. This time her heart raced, she felt dizzy. Her vision blurred but she reached for the window control button and commanded it to seal off the offensive odor.

After several deep breaths, "Jeremy is there anything to drink in here?"

"Yes, M'a— Ms. Bodin, in that compartment to the right, I think you'll find it sufficient to your needs."

An unopened bottle of Grand Marnier shimmered. She twisted the cap and poured a generous snifter full. She indulged with two big gulps and the knot threatening to close off her esophagus rendered. Alcohol had little to no effect on her but she loved the taste. It irritated Jeff to no end because he couldn't handle alcohol at all. The thought of Jeff made her a blush. They had been together for 15 years but Rose could not bring herself to tell him how she truly felt about him. She feared it would somehow cause conflict with the business part of their relationship, publicist and author. Besides, how could he or any man feel anything romantic for a woman with her baggage?

Chapter Two

ose chuckled out loud, *so, this is what southern hospitality looks like!* The luxurious suite definitely had everything she needed: a sitting area, desk, a fully stocked wet bar and a separate master bedroom.

Some of the dives she had stayed in when she was first published didn't have hot water, let alone Ethernet connections/WiFi and phone jacks. Jeff threatened to send her on a book signing at K-mart during a blue light special for Bic pens if it would've meant book sales.

Rose unpacked and took out a few of the snacks she liked to carry with her on trips, things she wasn't sure she could get away from home like her favorite brand of cherry licorice.

Rose took out the business card JoAnne had given her and sneered at the bold black letters, Sonny James, IV, Esquire.

"Esquire my ass, you're an attorney no matter what you call yourself." She threw the card onto the top of the desk, tossed her head back, shook her long wavy brown hair out of the scrunchie and pressed her fists tight against her temples and groaned, "Dammit! I've only been here a few minutes and I'm already tense."

Writing always cleared the funk. She set her laptop on the desk plugged it in, switched it on and began to type:

I will not burn! He clung to an abandoned fence post, gasped for air. Blood-sweat droplets glistened against decaying skin. The hunters' familiarity with the woods gave them ground. A baying hound signaled their approach. *Blood, I need blood!*

Images of scorching flames singed his thoughts as tiny rays of sunlight pierced through the leaves of an oak tree to burn his dried and browning flesh. *Focus!*

With drying eyes, flaking skin and crumbling fingertips he made his way to a huge Magnolia tree that spread its deep waxy leaves and overlapping limbs across the upper terrace of a sprawling Rose garden. No sunlight penetrated the trees' sanctuary. The air underneath became musty with decaying leaves on top of the moist, soft earth. He rolled in the dirt cooling his dehydrated flesh. Then, he heard it, the sweet, melodic voice of a child.

"Daddy's gone a huntin' to catch a lil' rabbit skin to wrap his lil' bundtin' in."

He slid his tongue out into the air, retrieved her scent and swallowed, hard. Hunger burned a path from his throat to his gut. He could not leave a corpse with the hunter so close.

So hungry, need blood. A ball burst into his shadowy lair. The flick of his wrist forced the ball back without the benefit of touch. He parted the limbs of the tree with less effort to see the tiny human approach with the confidence of his equal. She felt no fear he would've smelled it. Her eyes met his. She smiled, spreading the thin red mustache of Kool-Aid. She glared at the ball suspended above his palm.

"How'd ya—"

Big blue/grey eyes glistened in the rays of the setting sun. Her cheeks flush from play highlighted her olive complexion while strings of sweaty hair laid about her shoulders gathered at the corner of her mouth. He could smell the blood feast within her. He released the ball and waved his fingers in front of the girl's eyes. They glazed over as all his victims' had.

A gurgle erupted in his throat, an excitement he knew he had to control. To take the life of a child had consequences. All he wanted, needed, just enough blood to give him the strength to escape the hunters. A howled alert; *Hurry! I will be careful.*

He scooped her up and cradled her in his right arm. Her head rolled back over his bicep; her thick blood coursed through the throbbing blue jugular as it pulsed a sympathetic rhythm. His bloodlust boiled.

He whispered in her ear, "I am Constantine."

Then he sank his yellowed fangs into her tender, young neck. The skin yielded to him out of pity and the blood flowed in currents. His vision cleared, his skin plumped and his hair smoothed into a mane of ebony. Her vital blood brought colorful visions to his mind, her short life already filled with happiness, overwhelming contentment and beauty. The images contained inside this precious girls' heart became unbearable for him to witness he had to stop. *Ecstasy!*

A moan from deep inside her warned he may have gone too far, taken too much. The girl lay still in his arms her heart hovering at the abyss. *Think!* He bit his own lip and pressed the bloody flesh against her mouth. She gagged at first but within a few seconds she swallowed the life changing drops of blood. He pulled away. He feared giving her more than her little body could take, he couldn't change her that would be; he said the word out loud, "sacrilege."

Her eyes fluttered open as she licked her lips. "I'm Rose."

"Shhhh," he whispered. His restored finger outlined her now ruby red lips. She closed her eyes, content, and drifted off.

He rested her warm body against the tree. The wound had already begun to heal. He stood ready to take flight against the

now sunless, amber sky. He looked back at the sleeping child and
felt something he'd never felt before. Love, compassion, he could
not be sure but he did know that he would be back for her as soon
as he was free of the hunters.

After several hours of working Rose read what she'd written. Well done
she thought as she glanced at the time on the clock/radio, she consulted her
watch Atlanta was one hour ahead of Texas.

No wonder. Rose went down the service elevator she was brought up on
and approached the concierge's desk in the lobby. She wanted to know more
about the Crimson Café that was to host her book signing later in the evening.

"Excuse me. I need to get some information on a local coffee house."

"Yeah, which one?" Jeremy did not look up from the mini-TV that held
him captive.

"Crimson Café."

He looked up with a jerk, yanked at tangled earphones and stood to attention straightening his uniform vest with one hand.

"Ms. Bodin, my apologies, Ma'am, I didn't know it was you, oh, sorry for
the Ma'am." He cleared his throat, "Crimson Cafe, it's a hangout for young
gothic types but they only show up late night. During the day they serve coffee
and such to the folks who work downtown. I take my breaks there."

They discussed the history of the coffeehouse, how it had been open only
a few years. Once, an old hat shop, pre-civil war, and a triage post during the
civil war, it was now registered with the historical society. The new owner
agreed to absorb all cost of renovations in exchange for the historical record-
ing of the property and its' future preservation for which a healthy trust was
put into place.

"If there is ever anything you want to know about the Crimson Café or
any other place in Atlanta, I'm your huckleberry. If I don't know, I'll find
someone who does."

"Thank you, Jeremy, I appreciate your help. How far is the café from here?"

"It's a block and a half east. You could walk." He frowned. "But I guess that wouldn't be a good idea at night. As part of my duty and my personal pleasure," Jeremy put his hand over his heart, "I would be honored to escort you to the book signing?"

"That'd be nice, thank you. I'll see you tonight, around eight thirty." She took several steps toward the elevators stopped, looked back and said, "By the way, the rose is a nice touch, I like it." Rose turned and from behind her she heard a faint, 'Yes', from Jeremy.

"*Dead of Night*", the next book in the Constantine series, was already being talked about by some as the "best yet". What ideas bounced around in the dark recesses of her mind would have to develop soon or the ending of the book would be a total let down.

She was about to open the welcome basket, on the bar, when a knock at the door made her jump.

Why the hell am I so jumpy?

She opened the door to see Jeremy's beaming face.

"I spoke to the manager at Crimson's and she said we need to go in around back. She doesn't want a riot on her hands." Jeremy took a deep breath.

Rose chuckled at the young man's enthusiasm. "Is the café open?"

Jeremy's smile broadened, "They closed, at 10:30 this morning just to get ready for tonight, they'll reopen at "sundown", he made the quotation marks with his fingers, "whatever that means."

"Well, then, I guess I need to get some sleep. I'll see you around 8."

Jeremy just stood there with a huge grin on his face nodding. Rose motioned to shut the door and he moved slightly. "Thanks again, goodnight."

Rose shut the door, looked out the peephole and watched as Jeremy danced his way to the elevator. *Now that's a fan.*

Rose stretched and yawned she could feel how high the sun burned in the sky. The clock told her it was time to get some sleep. Napping during the hottest part of the day kept Rose safe and had now become a way of life for her. She cuddled up on top of the comforter and grabbed a throw to cover her feet. The cold pillow made her yawn again. *Oh, I'm tired.* Her cell phone dinged with a message. Lazily she reached across and grabbed it from the nightstand. It beamed "unknown caller" she clicked to read the text, "Welcome Home Rose".

Thoughts bantered, everyone knows I'm here but no one, outside Jeremy, should have my cell. *Maybe one of the reporters got wind of the other reason I'm in Atlanta. The letter from the attorney said this was just a formality so I could take possession of what was rightfully mine and that my birth mother must be in serious condition for them to take action now. Did she give me away because I was so different? Did she know what was wrong with me?*

Rose drifted off to sleep with questions still dancing in her mind. Music began to flow and she could feel herself gliding on air. Voices whispered all around her as she spun faster and deeper into the abyss of sleep. She sensed people staring but everything was out of focus. Without warning the music stopped, lights dimmed to a flicker. She turned and found herself face to face with Constantine. He looked exactly as she had described him in her books. Tall, jet-black hair and red-rimmed eyes, but this dream version was prettier and smoother. He smiled at her exposing his pristine, white fangs. He lifted his long, lean finger to her face and placed his sharp nail to her temple; ran it down to her throat, locked his eyes on hers and whispered, "Welcome home Rose."

He kissed her on the forehead. She quivered at the icy coldness of his lips. He pressed his lips to hers as his tongue made its' way into her mouth. At first, her body heaved into him she didn't want him to stop. Within seconds his tongue swelled filling her mouth, she gagged and tried to pull away but she couldn't move. He had her in a tight grip. Her eyes opened wide as Constantine's face began to distort. His eyes filled with blackness and his skin darkened to a brown dullness. Flakes of skin began to fall from his forehead. She gagged violently and used both hands against him in an effort to push away. When that didn't work, she hit him with both fists repeatedly in the chest. He moaned! He was enjoying this. He fed off her pain! Rose tried to scream but could only produce a whimper as tears ran down her face. In the distance she could hear a woman saying something. Not sure what, Rose concentrated on the melodic voice. It wasn't talk. The woman was singing a lullaby. Rose went limp. Constantine let her fall. She kept falling until she reached out with both hands to grab the darkness.

Rose found herself tangled in the comforter in a bundle on the floor. She quickly pulled off the covers and jumped to her feet. Her body still quivering with fear a wayward drop of sweat ran down her back. Rose stumbled into the bathroom.

She leaned over the sink to rinse her mouth. Her spit had blood tainted foam. Frantically she brushed her teeth and wiped at her mouth with a washcloth. When she examined her tongue she could see the blood ooze from two tiny punctures. She rinsed harder until clear water came out.

"Damn!" she exclaimed thinking she must have bit her tongue when she fell off the bed. Her dream went into the diary first then she would find a way to incorporate it into her vampire Constantine novels, that whole tongue swelling thing was gross. *My fans are gonna love this.*

Rose ordered up room service and passed the time by writing every detail she could remember about the dream. The kind of details that kept her stories fresh; the smell of wax that had burned too long, the feel of Constantine's cold dead skin against her. Rose welcomed these dreams, the images, because she felt they were part of her subconscious continuing the stories she had already set in motion. She let her mind wander then pounded the keys into submission. The night terrors were the dreams she couldn't remember like most of her childhood. Darkness just darkness a black hole in the center of her mind that she had to navigate tenderly while trying to remember lest she fall into it and be gone forever. Her memories could only go as far back as six years old. She was at a birthday party when a bully held her hand out a patio window into the harsh sun until it burned her skin. Rose would say, 'it was like that was the day I was born. I woke up." Although the boy died mysteriously, a few weeks later, from some strange fever no one could diagnose. Rose spent several weeks in Children's hospital for testing that determined along with her allergy to the Magnolia, she was also allergic to sunlight.

JoAnne home schooled Rose after that and introduced her to a whole new world through books. The first vampire book she read, Bram Stoker's

Dracula, filled her with hope. From that day on she read every vampire book available and watched every movie and T.V. show. She was hooked the first time she saw Barnabas Collins pine for his Josette. Nostferatu, the Vampyre became her favorite because it was about a real person who lived as a vampire. She had dreamt up Constantine by age fourteen. So, by the time she had finished high school, home school style, she was ready to start writing full time. And write is what she did. By 22 she had her first of 12 New York Times Bestsellers.

After a light dinner of sushi Rose felt a twinge of excitement about getting to the café. That queasy feeling in her gut, the one she always got right before a public appearance, reminded her of why she bothered with these appearances and that she was human. Her fans gave her strength and none of them cared if she was different, they loved her eccentricities. Other people judged her with long stares. Her olive skin, bright, blue/grey eyes and brown hair gave no indication that she was different. She learned to take precautions against people who mocked her. Her lifestyle was that of a night owl and she scheduled all book signings and appearances at nine p.m. or later. Of course, that only fed the supernatural nature of the books and fans ate it up.

A loud anxious knock caused Rose to jump up from her seat. Heart pounding, she peeked through the peephole. Jeremy stood in the hall. Well, he pranced around in the hallway. As the door began to open; he started, "Ms. Bodin, we need to get going. I talked to the owner at the café, Rebekah, she said it's a mob scene and we need to come in through the back alley as planned but that you might want to get there early."

"Okay, Jeremy, I need to grab a few things. I'll meet you at the elevator." Rose grabbed her bag and a wrap.

"Yes, Ma'—, Ms. Bodin." And with that he shuffled off.

Rose met Jeremy at the service elevator that took them uninterrupted to the parking garage. They had just rounded the corner when a striking gentleman stepped into their path. The statuesque man commanded attention in his starched uniform. A badge on the left side of his chest read Fulton County Sheriff. The pleats of his khaki pants were pressed sharp enough to cut, if someone was inclined to get that close. From his burr haircut and Stetson hat to his shiny black boots he could pass muster with the toughest of drill sergeants.

"Pardon, me." He took a step back.

Jeremy tried to hide his fear by looking at the ground but his voice cracked, "Hi, Uncle Bo. What are you doing here?"

"Official business, but I saw you got your pick-up so mudded you can't make out the license plate. That's a good way to get —" he paused, removed his gold aviator sunglasses folded them and placed them gingerly in his shirt pocket. Graying eyebrows scrunched tight deepening the crevices that furrowed his forehead, his hazel eyes glared down at Rose.

The sheriff towered over her. She extended her hand upwards, "I'm Rose Bodin."

"Ms. Bodin." He put a finger to the rim of his hat and tipped it ever so slight then took her hand, "Sheriff James Boregard Hayden, it's nice to meet you. I was just on my way up to visit with you."

"She's a famous author, what would you have to talk to her about?" Jeremy recoiled at the realization he'd spoken out of turn and looked at the beetle bug crawling across the concrete.

Rose assumed the wound-too-tight sheriff wanted an autograph, "If it's not urgent, which I can't imagine it is, can we meet later or tomorrow? I need to get to my book signing."

The Sheriff stared back motionless for several seconds. He nodded in acceptance and replaced his glasses. "It can wait."

Rose grinned as an image took shape of the Sheriff's badge number tattooed on his ass. *I'll have to use that in my next book.*

"You two be careful out there. Jeremy, get your tags cleaned off."

As if on cue, the elevator doors opened, the Sheriff stepped in. Rose and Jeremy stood silent until the elevator displayed that several floors had passed.

Jeremy wiped beads of sweat from his forehead, "It's like he's just waiting for an excuse to shoot somebody."

"We need to go." Rose motioned to her Tag watch, a gift from her mother, which she valued as much as her time.

They passed Jeremy's black Ford F-350 Duely. Rose could see the thick, red Georgia mud under the wheel well was growing stalactites.

The tinting on the back window wasn't enough to hide the empty gun rack but a sticker warned, ***THIS VEHICLE PROTECTED BY SMITH-WESSON.***

Cowboys in Texas would be envious.

It made her feel safe, a feeling she wasn't accustom to away from home. They exchanged idle chatter for several minutes. But as they walked through a dark delivery alley, the thought occurred to Rose that Jeremy might know a private investigator that could get her the information she wanted about her birth parents, someone other than the attorney, Sonny James IV.

"How many family members do you have in law enforcement?"

"More than I care to admit to. Uncle Bo is my dad's younger brother. My dad is a Chief at Firehouse 10."

"Would you know a private investigator that could do some work for me while I'm here?"

"Yes."

She touched his arm, "I need to get some information on a delicate matter and I'd prefer a professional to handle it for me."

"I got ya', incognito," he winked and placed his hand over hers.

"Exactly," Rose slid her long thin fingers out from under Jeremy's hand and smiled.

"I have another uncle, Don Coleman from my mom's side of the family. Everybody calls him DC. I'll give him a call while you're autographing books."

"Thanks Jeremy. If he's available to come to the hotel tomorrow night, seven-ish, that'd be great."

"I'll see what I can do."

Rose sighed. A rush of cold air brought out goose bumps on her arms. She shivered and began to rub her bare arms.

Jeremy put a firm, warm hand on her back, "You're cold."

"I just got a chill. I'll be fine. I have my wrap it should be enough."

"My grandmother says when you shiver for no reason it means someone just walked over the spot where you'll be buried. Creepy, huh?"

Rose nodded but kept walking. She thought about the shivers and a feeling of being watched caught up to her.

They crossed into the glaring light of a single exposed bulb hanging next to the café door. Rose could feel her heart quicken and her breath catch. Every pore on her head tingled when there in front of her stood a shadow.

Chapter Three

Arms reached out of the shadow, grabbed Rose by the shoulders and pulled her over the threshold. The woman hugged her like a long lost relative. Rose grunted under the pressure.

The woman pulled away, huge deep brown eyes danced, she squealed, "I'm Rebekah Cantu. I'm so excited to meet you I think I could just burst." The woman shook like a kid on Christmas morning.

Rose inhaled a nostril full of perfume that knotted and twisted her gut. The scent filled her with a familiar sweet sickness that made her dizzy. *Magnolia!*

She reached out and fanned at the air.

Rebekah braced her, "Steady, hon, don't want you to pass out before you've signed some books. My God, you're a waif of a woman aren't you? You need some good ole Southern cooking, a pot of collard greens and pork chops 'll put some meat on your bones."

"I'll be fine. It's just, your perfume is . . ." She shook her head, "It reminds me of something. What is it?"

With a fanning motion so as to spread the aroma the café owner grinned. "It's a mixture of lavender, magnolia, a touch of cloves and my own little secret ingredient." She tilted her head and winked, "if you like it, I'll share. I make this stuff by the vat."

"That'd be very generous of you but . . ." Rose stopped, not wanting to offend her hostess she accepted the generous offer.

The café felt damp and musty like a cellar not a bookstore or a coffee house. Something she couldn't put her finger on made the place feel decrepit and off. Books behind the solid oak bar that ran the width of the place looked to be especially old and valuable. A strange vine grew up one corner by the door and made its' way halfway across the ceiling. It bore some kind of purple fruit but not exactly grapes.

"What kind of plant is that?"

"It's a Muscadine vine. When we began renovations, it was growing wild right outta the floor. It was so determined to live that I just had to let it into the scheme."

"Nice."

"It makes a great wine too. When my great-great-great grandparents arrived here they fell in love with the grape. They used a centuries old wine method that the family used back in the old country. They have a winery now in Nachez, Mississippi. My cousins run it but I prefer the big city. Have a seat I'll bring you a glass to sample. If you like I can send some home with you." Rebekah turned and sauntered toward the bar.

"Sounds good. Thank you." Rose replied almost as an after-thought. On the wall opposite the door was a mural. A painting of a civil war battle with a huge plantation on fire in the background. Animals were fleeing a fully engulfed barn as a group of angry men with guns hunted a dark figure. Hounds foamed at the mouth as they alerted the men to their prey. Rose took in every detail of the mural. She could almost hear the shouts of men and the baying of hounds. In the bottom right corner in deep rich green hues a huge Magnolia tree. The blossoms looked real enough to touch. She could almost smell their nectar, sweet and thick. It made her swallow hard and turn away.

Rebekah patted Rose on the back, "It's kinda creepy, huh? The owner commissioned the mural and then detailed it himself. I think it's wild and vicious, don't you?" She said with her eyes wide. "Here's your wine, have a seat and let me know if I can get you anything else." Then she was off, making last minute adjustments on her way to open the door.

A couple of hours into the book signing Rose looked up to motion for Rebekah but noticed a man standing at one end of the bar. She couldn't make out all his features but something about him seemed familiar. He had to be more than six feet tall with broad shoulders and freshly coiffed jet-black hair tied neatly into a ponytail with a black satin ribbon. An animal magnetism surrounded him, oozed from every pore of his porcelain skin. Rose maneuvered herself to get a look at his face and her nipples tingled. She closed her eyes allowing the warm feeling to advance but when she opened them, the man was gone. She motioned for Rebekah, again.

"You look a little peaked. How about some of my famous sweet tea? You'll love it. You're almost done sweetie, which is a good thing 'cause we're about outta' books."

"If you e-mail Jeff now, I'll bet he'll over-night a shipment to you. By the way, there was a man standing at the bar a minute ago, did you…"

One lady in line interrupted, "It's so exciting."

An older gentleman touted— "Be it Texas or Georgia you can take the girl outta the south but you can't never take the south outta the girl."

Rebekah spun around the ends of her white eyelet skirt flipped. On her ankle Rose noticed a tattoo, a large red drop of blood.

"You're right," Rose signed the man's book, *from one Southerner to another* and posed with him for a photo.

Rose eyed the long line of fans and near to the door she made eye contact with the strange man she had seen at the bar. The piercing blackness of his eyes seared through to her soul. It made her feel naked and exposed. Her ears began to ring and her skin burned as the room closed in. A tingling coldness invaded her skin beginning from her heart. A sudden flash blinded her. She blinked several times. He vanished, again.

"Thank ya', Ms. Bodin, my wife's gonna love this photo." The man patted his camera and left with his book.

Rose managed to get through the rest of the night but couldn't shake the feeling of being off balance.

After saying goodbye to the last customer, Rebekah closed up shop. At the bar, Jeremy and a young man were having a heated conversation about Atlanta's prized college football team.

"Jeremy, are you old enough to drink that?" Rose asked with a grin.

He stammered a little, "I-I may look young but that's 'cause I got good genes. Speaking of genes, my uncle, DC said he'd be glad to meet you tomorrow in the hotel bar."

"Great." *Now I can get what I need and get out of here before the press gets wind of my agenda.*

On the bar sat an opened and dusty bottle of Grand Marnier.

"Is this the two-hundred-year-old?" Rose tilted the bottle.

"I think I've had it that long, help yourself," Rebekah handed her a snifter.

Rose poured the liquid and drew in a deep breath to keep from inhaling the sharp fumes and took a sip. "Mmm, almost as good as sweet tea. Rebekah, that tattoo on your ankle, it looks like a drop of blood?"

"Oh, that ole thing," she lifted her leg behind her to show the inked art. "It's my inspiration. As a child I nearly bled to death 'cause of hemophilia. But, after a transfusion I was miraculously cured. So, I got this to remind me every day that every drop is precious." She winked and went about putting up chairs.

After several rounds of drinks and some laughs Rose got up to go to the restroom. She could feel the effects of the jet lag and the stress but she never felt drunk. Rose had a resistance to alcohol but not to Rebekah's oily perfume it had begun to take its' toll. Rose could feel it seeping into her pores leaving her skin tacky. She looked into the mirror that hung over the sink by a lacy blue ribbon.

"Damn, I look like the living dead."

Her blue/grey eyes had dulled and pink invaded the tender skin around the edges. Her makeup had worn off and left her skin-tone pale and ruddy. She bent over the basin to dab cold water on her face. Chills, like sharp fingernails dipped in ice, clawed their way up her spine. The breath she let out hung in the air above the water, the temperature in the small room had dropped to near freezing. When she looked up to see the reflection of the strange man she saw earlier, Rose turned on her heels so fast she lost her balance, grabbed the edge of the sink as she went down landing on the floor solid on her butt. She jumped up still holding on to the sink with both hands and looked into the mirror again. Hers was the only image.

I must be tired.

Rose rubbed her temples, took a deep breath and straightened her blouse. She walked back to the bar and put her hands up in surrender. "I'm tired, time to say good-night."

Jeremy and Rose made their way back to the hotel under a purple-black sky blanketed with a trillion brilliant stars and one pair of blood rimmed eyes.

Chapter Four

Rose fumbled for the ringing phone, knocked over a can of soda then grabbed the noisy assailant. The mechanical voice on the other end announced the 5 p.m. wake-up call she had ordered. Taking a few deep breaths she tossed the covers aside, sat up and put both feet on the floor. Rose put her head in her hands and let an expletive escape with a heavy exhale.

"Dammit, I feel like a two-hundred-year-old wash rag left out to dry."

After cleaning up the soda with a pillowcase she gulped what remained in the can of soda then tossed it into the trash on her way to the bathroom.

Rose pulled off the blouse she had slept in. It reeked of cigar smoke mingled with Rebekah's perfume calling to mind the image of the man she'd seen three different times. Rose turned on the water and stepped into the steamy shower. She chose the lemongrass scented shower gel and lathered every inch of her perfectly toned body. She didn't have a flaw, at least, not that she'd found. Rose knew it had to be genetics because she hadn't worked out a day in her life. The water's pressure was perfect as it pounded the remaining scant of makeup from her face. The washcloth felt amazing as it stripped away the layers of the day before. She rested her forehead against the cold tile and pulled on the showerhead until the water made a river from the base of her neck, her back, and finally down her legs. She felt a presence then a chill.

She called out. "Who's there?"

No one answered.

She rinsed and set about the task of washing her shoulder length hair. She kept it trimmed because it grew quickly. She felt a firm icy touch on her hip. Fist in the air and soap in her eyes she spun around. Her heel tangled with the shower curtain and sent her crashing hard to the bottom of the tub.

"Ooh shit! Get a grip," she commanded, breaking the silence. After she exited the shower, nude, and inspected the entire suite she believed the whole incident to be a product of her overly active imagination. Then, she gingerly rubbed her hip. "That's gonna leave a mark."

Rose turned off the shower and donned her favorite chenille robe. Her computer began to ding with an instant message.

"Jeff!" relieved Rose chuckled at her giddy reaction.

> *Hey, how did things go? Rebekah ordered more books, said things went great for her but I'd like to hear from you.*
>
> *Jeff*

Rose replied:

> *I don't know how you found this place but it was filled with fans. I'll get back to you later have a few things to take care of. R.*

Looking out the huge picture window of the hotel lounge Rose watched as a squatty man tried, with no success, to console a woman. The man accepted a hearty slap across his robust cheek as the woman turned to leave, in a huff. The man pouted, spotting Rose, he waved. She looked around then realized he was waving at her. She pointed to herself with a look of confusion.

He mouthed. "Are you Rose?"

Nodding an affirmative she rolled her eyes and motioned for him to join her as she looked at her watch, half past eight, he was late.

His suit, wrinkled and stained, looked like he'd slept in it for days. Sweat rings around the collar and the underarms added to the overall disheveled appearance.

His hands shook as he introduced himself, "Mizz Bodin, I'm Don Coleman, just call me DC, everybody does." He sat in the chair directly across from Rose. "Thank God for nightfall, it was a hot one out there today, for spring that is, but I'll take it any day over the cold." He removed his pale-yellow cotton hat and began to fan his red swollen face. "My nephew said you needed some help of a personal and confidential nature, well, let me tell you, I'm your man."

"Would you like some tea?" Rose interrupted for fear the man would stroke out before getting some relief.

"Sweet tea, please, ma'am." With that, Rose motioned to the waitress.

Without skipping a beat, he continued with his promotional campaign. "As I was saying, I'm your man. I come from a long line of law enforcers. My daddy was with the Atlanta K-9 division for 35 years before he was shot to death by a good for nothin' scumbag in our own home."

He took one quick breath, "And my granddaddy was a Sheriff for Fulton County. My aunts, uncles and most other kin are in some form of law enforcement or government. They got good benefits those government jobs do. 'Course you already met my nephew, Jeremy. He's real smart, college boy, if you know what I mean." He winked. "Kinfolk make for good contacts when I need information so whatever it is you can count on DC to get the job done."

He stopped for a drink of the tea he took out of the waitresses' hand.

Rose jumped in, "That's a pretty impressive list of relatives. I need information about an adoption ..." Before she could finish, DC started up again.

"Right up my alley, got a cousin, Georgie, well, he just got divorced but his ex-wife has a girlfriend, that didn't surprise anyone but Georgie, she works in vital statistics at the courthouse. Nice girl before she went and turned gay. But, that's ancient history. Tell me everything you know about the child you gave up." DC put both elbows on the table and focused his attention on Rose. She glared at the offending appendages and he promptly removed them.

Rose drew in a deep breath, "It's not like that," she pointed to herself, "I was adopted and I need to get some information about my birth parents."

DC leaned back in his chair and crossed his legs but he kicked the table knocking over his tea, "Oh, my apologies." Bare handed with open palms, he swept the excess from the table onto the plush carpet. The waitress dashed over with a bar towel and vowed to return with a fresh tea.

Rose pulled her Ostrich skin bag from under the table and safely away from the sugar-laden drink. "To be specific, I need to know my birthparents' medical history and the events surrounding my adoption." She retrieved a manila folder, "I know my birth mother is living but she's in some sort of institution. I've made a list of a few questions I really need answers to and a list of contacts, including the estate attorney, Sonny James, IV."

DC took the folder and began scanning the pages, "Easy enough, Mr. James should have most of this information at his disposal. He's got roots in Atlanta go back to the Civil War and then some. You could call him yourself. He's probably got all the answers you need."

The waitress returned with a fresh drink in a Styrofoam cup with a lid and a straw. Rose smiled as the waitress turned in her direction with a wink.

Rose leaned over the table a bit, "I have an appointment to meet him but I would prefer to have this information before I meet with him. I prefer to have someone less bias working from another angle." Rose pointed to the papers. "I know I was born in Georgia Baptist Hospital on June 5, 1965. My birth name was Agnes Rose Harris. My adoptive parents gave me the name Rose Anne Bodin. How quick do you think you can find out something?" She sat back in her seat and folded her arms.

"Of course, tomorrow being Sunday and all," DC fidgeted, wiped his forehead with his sleeve, "it could be Monday before I can get anything to go on. You could look this stuff up yourself, why use someone like me?"

"That's okay, I'm not scheduled to return to Texas until Thursday, but if I need to stay longer I will. I need answers. I also need this kept quiet, which is another reason I'm not doing the research on my own. If you get an inkling the press is on to this please, let me know right away."

"Gotch ya', now there's the matter of my fee. I charge $300.00 dollars a day plus expenses, except Sundays. I don't usually work on Sundays, with all the government offices being closed, but I'll make an exception, this once. After all, Jeremy did recommend me and I want to make a good showing. You'll get a typed detailed report when I'm done, with documentation, like copies of death certificates and stuff. I'm good at what I do Ms. Bodin, you can count on me."

"I hope so. Your fee is acceptable and I'll pay you a bonus of $500.00 if you can make this a priority and get me what I need by Wednesday."

He stood up, "I'll be in touch." He handed Rose one of his business cards, "Oh, and thanks for the tea. It was real nice."

Rose watched as the man made his way through the lobby and out the doors only to bump into a woman, knocking her to the ground.

What the hell have I done?

⸻ ✦✦✦✦✦ ⸻

Back in her room Rose decided to call her mom. She hadn't talked to her since she and JoAnne had argued about whether she should claim her biological family's inheritance. The phone only rang twice when the familiar raspy voice answered, "Bodin residence, JoAnne speaking"

"Hi, Mom."

"Rose? Is that you?"

"Okay. I'm sorry I didn't call sooner."

"Me too, kitten."

"I'm here in Atlanta."

"Jeffery mentioned it when he called yesterday."

"Jeffery called you? What for?"

"He's worried about you. And, the Crystal Ball is coming up. I think he's buttering me up for a ticket."

"Don't worry Mom and I'm sure you're right, he loves the gala."

"Don't worry, is that all you choose to say to your dear ole mother? You work too much. I know that no matter how little sleep you get you work too much. Besides, I'm concerned about you taking pills. There are all kinds of studies showing the dangers of . . ."

"Mom, please, they're prescription." *Thanks Jeff.* "My doctor is looking out for me. I didn't call to discuss that, anyway. I called to let you know I'm in Atlanta and I'm going to try see my birth mother."

Rose didn't mean to blurt it out like that but there it was. JoAnne knew the reason for the visit but to have it put in her face so sharply couldn't have been easy. And, when there was no reaction, Rose licked her parched lips and continued, "I have to get a handle on this before the press does. It could ruin everything. Who knows how this could play out or how it could affect my career. I just have to find out all the information I can about my birthmother before the press does. Besides, maybe my sun sensitivity is genetic. And, she might be able to fill in the gaps of my childhood, the dark part I can't remember. Knowing you were adopted is one thing knowing you're about to meet the woman who gave you up is something all-together different. I didn't expect this kind of —"

Silence filled the distance between them.

JoAnne's voice cracked a little. "It's not like I didn't know this day would come. You need to know all you can about where and who you came from."

Rose could hear the double click of the lighter and deep draw of breath as her mom lit a cigarette and took her first signature long drag. Rose could visualize her mother's eyes as they closed and twitched with the final exhalation of the nicotine-laced smoke.

"I wish I had more answers for you, but we weren't given much. I think it's good you're reaching out. But, kitten, she may not be what you have imagined. If you need me. I'll be here." JoAnne paused to inhale more nicotine. "Rose, I love you."

"I love you, more. Thanks, mom, for understanding. I wouldn't want to hurt you."

"I know. That's not what this is about. You need to do what you need to do. Don't work too late." JoAnne made the usual kissing sound. Then came the silent tone.

The talk with her mom had put her at ease like she knew it would.

Rose felt energized and pounded away at the laptop chewing on red licorice for inspiration. The keys hummed and the cursor flew. Halfway through a sentence Rose switched to her e-mail option and chided Jeff for his shameless attempt at getting an invite from her mother. And then she let him know he could have the honor of escorting her to the Crystal Ball but he had to wear the monkey suit.

Rose's cell phone rang. "Yes Jeff?"

"Rose, I just~"

Not letting him finish, "hey, I sent you an e-mail, did you get it?"

"Not yet, I called because I thought we could really take advantage of your time in Atlanta."

"How exactly do "we" do that?"

"I set up a couple of interviews for you to talk about 'Crimson'."

"Interviews with who?"

"A nationally syndicated radio show and a reporter with the Atlanta Journal-Constitution."

"A radio interview?"

"Yes."

Silence.

Jeff cleared his throat. "Rose, are you there?"

"It's a morning show, isn't it? You know I don't do mornings. How early is this show, anyway?"

"Six a.m. tomorrow."

"What!"

"Don't get your thong in a wad its one radio show. C'mon, Rose, it can't possibly be that hard to get your ass out of bed one morning. In fact, you don't even have to get out of bed. I'm not asking you to greet the sun. You don't have to go outside. Hell! You don't have to get dressed. The production manager will call you and you can do it all by phone." He continued, as his confidence grew. "I don't care if you need a voodoo doctor with chicken bones and a witch with incense you need this interview, remember you are trying to throw off the scent of the press." He waited.

Rose held the phone in both her hands gripping it in a chokehold position. She spoke with a low guttural voice. "I suppose you'll reimburse me the cost of the voodoo doctor and a new thong? You owe me one Jeffery Cornell Robinson." And she hung up the phone. She knew he got the message because she only used his full name when she was really aggravated.

The details from the radio station about the interview came to her e-mail moments later. It was about one in the morning by the time Rose finished editing. She decided it was time to have a snack, some Kobi beef sliced thin. Raw meat and raw seafood were the one source of protein she could digest without agonizing discomfort and she had tried lots of different foods. Rose called herself a micro-biotic carnivore. Sugar was always good, especially in candy. Afterward, it was time to turn out all the lights except the desk lamp; a red silk scarf over it gave the room a pink glow. One last check of the triple layer blackout draperies and she slipped into her most comfortable T-shirt and took her sleeping pill. Lying on the bed with her head and shoulders on the pillows she began to relax.

She tensed and relaxed each muscle starting with her toes and worked her way up to the eyebrows. The pill took hold like a warm blanket. It slowed her breathing to match the weight on her chest. Her last conscious thought was of darkness, sweet caressing darkness.

Rose gasped for breath. Her heart echoed with the distant beat of another's. It over powered hers in moments. She was on a cliff overlooking a vast body of water. Waves crashed against the rocks below. A strange reverberation gave off a pinging sound in her ears. Icy sea spray hit her face. She managed to find her balance.

She squinted, struggled to focus. In the distance, the tree from her hypnosis-session or was it? The confusion overwhelmed her mind. *Think, it's just a dream!*

That's when she saw him standing by the Magnolia tree. Her eyes stung from the salt spray, everything blurred.

He motioned with long white fingers for her to come. The limbs parted to make a path. His voice melodic and unthreatening as words echoed in her head. She floated with a jerky motion like an 8 ml. film, her feet just inches from the ground, toward him.

She repeated over and over that it had to be a nightmare but she couldn't wake up. Again, the echo of a heartbeat, forceful and steady. As she gained ground, the heartbeats became undistinguishable.

Then, they were face to face.

She could feel the cold that radiated from his body. Her head became heavy as eyes yearned to close. She struggled to make out details of his face but he remained just a vague image with dark hair.

A familiar voice reverberated, "You cannot resist me."

She tried to scream. Her knees buckled. Instantly, arms secured around her waist. Though the grip chilled, Rose succumbed to its' power. Her head bobbed her body curled into his. Dead lips touched her neck with such tenderness that it sent a wave of passion through her body. *What hold does he have over me?*

It no longer mattered who this man was, just that he didn't stop. She welcomed his strength, his touch, his lips, everything. She desired him, she wanted to fight but it was useless. He licked her neck with a teasing flick of his tongue. She could feel tension build in his body. He grabbed a handful of her hair at the nape of her neck and yanked her head as far back as it could stand. The sheer force brought out a whimper from the deepest pit of her desires. He pressed his lips tight against her ear. "It is almost time."

The sensation of falling caused Rose's entire body to jerk, her arms grabbed at air. Still reeling from the effects of the sleeping pill Rose stared at the phone that had appeared in her hand and whispered in a hoarse voice. "Hello."

Chapter Five

"**D**C here, Ms. Bodin. I have located your birth mama. Unfortunately, she's in a mental hospital in Miledgeville. They won't let me near her. Family only or some shit. Pardon my French."

"What? My mother, you said something about my mother?" She pulled the phone close to her ear.

"Sorry, uh, I must'a woke you up. I figured you for an early bird. I can call back later. What time'd be good for you?"

"What about my mother?" Rose spoke with a little more authority.

"You know, the one you got me looking for."

"Oh, yeah," things began to click, "Sorry, I… what time is it?"

"It's exactly five fifty-eight a.m., early bird gets the worm, or birth-mother as in this case." He chuckled alone.

"Great, my wakeup call will be any second. Can I call you back later? I have to do some radio interview and I need to get some coffee, quick."

"You got it, Mizz Bodin."

Rose plopped the phone back on the cradle. She staggered from the chaise to start the coffee maker then made her way to the bathroom. At the sink she splashed cold water on her face and applied her usual face lotion.

Well at least no one can see you on radio.

She brushed her teeth and sat down by her desk with her first cup of coffee, the phone rang.

A young woman's voice chimed, "Good morning, Ms. Bodin, so glad you could be with us."

Oh, God, how can anyone be so damn chipper this early?

She heard the DJ in the background say, "And, we'll be right back with the author of the Vampire Constantine novels, Rose Bodin. Later, you can call our hit line to ask questions. Stay tuned."

After a short empty pause, a caffeine and cigarette fermented voice rasped, "Ms. Bodin, I'm Sandy and my husband is Ted. We're the morning show hosts. I'm sure you know how this works it can't be your first rodeo but we'll try to make it as painless as possible."

"It's early. Don't expect much," Rose sipped more coffee.

• • ✦ ✦ ✦ • •

By the time Rose had finished a second cup the DJ announced they'd take the last caller.

"The last caller says his name is, get this, Constantine. This ought to be fun. Go ahead caller you're on the line with Ms. Bodin." Sandy said, Ted chuckled.

Silence, then Rose heard a distant noise, a heartbeat. Her dream came back to her in a flood of tingling sensations.

"Hello caller, are you there?" The voice of the DJ slowed to a vibration in her ear. Each syllable echoed through time and space before landing back into the receiver.

Rose felt an icy shiver travel through her. She looked around the room, the furniture got fuzzy and the lights turned bright. Her head became so heavy it bobbed a little. A belch made its way up into her throat and flooded her mouth with the coopery taste of blood. A strange smell, sweet like perfume, it was on her hands, in her hair, the chenille robe, even the phone. Rose gagged. She wanted to stand but could only imagine the act. The room echoed with the heartbeat again and after each down beat the room became smaller. Then without warning everything reverted instantaneously back to regular speed, so fast it made her head jolt back and then bounce forward.

"I guess he chickened out. And that's all the time we have so I want to thank Ms. Bodin for taking our call."

"Thank you for having me," Rose heard the words but had no idea how she'd said them.

"Don't forget to look for her next book in the series *Midnight*."

The phone went dead and the weird feelings ceased, Rose stumbled as she got up.

Looking at the clock she moaned, "Aw, hell, I need to call DC." She decided to use her cell instead of the wacked out hotel phone.

"Yeah."

"DC, it's Rose."

"Hey."

"Sorry about before, I had to take the call from the radio station. You said something about my birth-mother and an institution?"

"Yeah, I figure if we get to Miledgeville tonight we can sleep over and be at the institution first thing Monday morning."

"Works for me."

Rose hung up the phone and crawled back under the covers. Closing her eyes, she slept in the safety of blackout draperies.

DC chatted on and on about his connections and how easy it was to locate her mother, "I'm glad you called. I wanted to get an early start in the morning, but ..." He paused to light a cigarette, "You don't mind, do you? I'll crack a window."

Rose shook her head. She was too busy thinking to respond verbally. I need to know what happened to me as a little girl. I need to focus and not get all caught-up in the mommy-I've-found-you-nonsense—

DC continued "... there ain't gonna be anything nice, not like you're use to. I found the deed online with a computer program I got called Title Box. Your Mamma has a real good attorney his secretary gave me a lot of the other information. But I did find a police report that was tucked away in a file. Well, my cousin found it. Credit where due and all."

Rose picked up her soda took a long swig and relaxed as the tip of the sun kissed the horizon good night.

"Have you been listening?" DC blew a puff of smoke toward the window.

"Sorta."

"As I was saying, Elizabeth has a damn good attorney, Sonny James the Fourth is one of a generation of James'. He hired a local guy by the name of Dwayne, just Dwayne, to look after the house. He's a Down Syndrome."

"You mean he has the genetic disorder called Down Syndrome." Rose put up her hands as if that alone shouted out, dumbass.

"Yeah, what I said, he's a Down Syndrome." DC flicked the rest of the cigarette out the window.

"The house ain't far from downtown, a neighborhood called the West End, real old money. Entrepreneurs have been buying up property left and right so they can build new. I put a call into Mr. James' office to get you a key but it was too early for him, too. I left a message."

Rose's stomach churned with anticipation. Was she more nervous about meeting her biological mother or the prospect of having to stay in Atlanta much longer with its eerie feelings and bad dreams? It gave Rose a headache to even think about it all so she closed her eyes and tried to clear her mind.

The neon lights of the no-tell-motel glowed with the anticipation of something seedy, but they had to stay somewhere and Mimi's Motel looked as good a place as any.

"Uh, DC, do you mind checking in for us, I don't want to be recognized."

"Don't mind at all. I'll use one of my many aliases." His eyes twinkled and his grin went crooked.

Rose handed him several large bills. "Hey that's an awful lot of money for a dive like this, but I'll take it."

DC returned and held out two room keys. "First pick."

Rose took one of the keys. "Thanks. What time can we get to the hospital?"

"8 a.m., so we'll need to pull out by ten of."

"What is it with everyone and getting up so early?"

"The nurse said your Mamma's more alert in the morning. Oh, before I forget, here's your packet."

Rose looked at the stuffed manila envelope and then at DC.

"What's this?"

"My bill and a copy of your birth certificate, military release records, receipts and stuff about the estate, including your grandmother's will. Some of it I downloaded from the Internet; but that police report is, well, it'll make for good bedtime reading. I figured it'll sink in better if you read it for yourself." He got out of the car and walked to his room. He turned back. "Don't forget to lock the car."

It took Rose several minutes of staring at the folder in complete silence before she realized she was alone in a parking lot near an asylum. Cold chills ran up and down her spine. She shook from the impact. The wives tale Jeremy's grandmother warned of shot through her mind. Rose squeezed the room key tight, grabbed her over-night bag and the envelope then locked the car doors before she headed to her room.

After she read all the documents in the folder Rose pulled out her cell phone charger and plugged it in, she wanted no interruption when she called her mother in Texas.

"Hi, mom."

"Kitten!" JoAnne squealed, "are you home?"

"No, I'm in Miledgeville, Georgia."

"What are you doing there?"

"Mom, do you know Sonny James the Fourth?"

"He's the attorney handling the property in Atlanta."

"Well, it seems his father, Sonny James the Third, was the one who orchestrated my adoption."

"It's been so many years, but yes that would be correct."

"I read the report from the private investigator I hired."

"You hired a private investigator? Why, Kitten? I'd tell you all you need to know."

"But not everything. It says my biological father, George W. Harris and my maternal grandmother, Emma Elizabeth Voss, were killed in a double homicide. The police report is a little sketchy it looks like it was hand written but there was a gun and a knife involved. My biological mother, Elizabeth Violet Harris, is in an asylum here in Miledgeville. You didn't tell me any of this."

A long pause, then her mother spoke. "That was so long ago. They keep some records hidden I had no way of knowing about all that."

Rose could hear the tapping of her mother's porcelain fingernails, and then the double -click of a lighter to ignite the long white Virginia Slim cigarette.

"Come on, Mom, you've got to tell me how it happened, because it obviously wasn't all cupcakes and sprinkles like you told me."

"It's not shady if that's what you mean. Your dad got a transfer to Fort Macpherson air base, near Atlanta." JoAnne exhaled, "He'd heard about a doctor who helped couples like us, couples who were having trouble getting pregnant. We'd been trying for so long, it looked hopeless. Then we got the results of our fertility tests, neither your dad nor I could ever conceive a child."

Rose hung her head, pulled the phone closer to her and tucked her knees against her chest. She could hear the disappointment in her mother's voice and the tinking of ice in her favorite crystal glass of vodka.

"Two weeks later your dad came home and found me with a fifth of gin and a bottle of pills."

"Mom, you didn't—"

"No, but I felt so useless, I wanted to die. Then late one evening, this attorney shows up on our doorstep. He says he's aware of our situation and he's a friend of our doctor. Well, after hearing what he had to say and conferring with our doctor, we signed the adoption papers. Two days later we got you."

"So, some strange guy shows up outta the blue and you agree to adopt some, what, 6 year-old kid sight unseen?"

"We were desperate, Kitten. For years after we looked over our shoulders afraid someone would take you back. Your dad put in for a transfer to NAS and he got it. So, we moved to Dallas. You weren't stolen. The attorney said he could expedite the adoption process because he was your legal guardian and all the papers checked out."

"I can't imagine what you went through, but didn't it occur to you to ask why?"

"No. I could finally have the little girl I'd always dreamt of. And, you looked so sad and empty with those sad kitten eyes you looked like so lost. The moment I saw you, you were mine."

"I'm going to meet the woman who gave birth to me. I will find out about my genetics. Are you sure there is nothing else I need to know?"

"No. You do what you have to and when you get home we'll go to the club for a long leisurely lunch. I love you."

"I love you too, Mom. Sleep good and sorry it's so late."

"I'm used to it, night-night." And as always, she made a kissing sound into the phone.

Chapter Six

The next morning Rose and DC pulled up to the quaint hospital surrounded by the most extravagant rose gardens and lush fruit trees. There were pears, figs and several varieties of apples. Magnolias dotted the landscape in clusters. Kudzu grew up every available space that wasn't pruned. The day was overcast and cloudy, rain misted on everything making the green of the grass a green Rose had never seen.

There were vacant sitting areas in front of the circle driver. The white columns made it look like an old Antebellum home but the bared windows and squared off corners could not be mistaken for anything but a hospital.

Rose asked, "DC, do you mind if I go this alone. I'm not sure what to expect."

DC rolled down the car window and lit a cigarette. "Fine with me, I don't care too much for hospitals. All that blood floatin' around, it's too spooky for my taste but here you might need these." He handed her a folder. "It's some added details I came across last night it might come in handy in there."

Rose pulled the floral silk scarf tighter around her neck to protect the last bit of delicate skin from the sun, and exited the car. Swings littered the broad front porch, along with potted ferns and empty wheelchairs. Inside the front entry looked in keeping with the front façade. She could almost hear Scarlett yelling after Rhett Butler, "Well, I do give a damn!" *Oh, that's going in a book.*

The green front doors opened into a busy lobby area with doctors and nurses buzzing about talking with people who looked perfectly sane but then Rose thought, *how does someone insane look?* She was reminded of the eyes she saw while at the book signing, black trimmed with red and blazing. That was insane, down right crazy. *Yeah, I gotta write this down.*

Rose sat on the overly stuffed large print sofa and dug for her pen and pad. She had just finished reading the cover sheet in the folder, her mind reeling from the information, when a stout nurse dressed in peach approached, extended her hand and called Rose by name. After the nurse admitted to being a fan, she introduced herself. Rose could not have remembered the woman's name if her life depended on it. The two walked down a long corridor passing several locked doors with security guards standing at each. At the end of the hall, a set of flimsy wooden doors seemed so inadequate for an asylum. They weren't even able to keep the sunlight out as it trickled in, around the edges and dust danced on the hardwood floor.

"Elizabeth's catatonic. She's happy to just rock back and forth, like she's rocking a real baby instead of that moldy rag doll." The nurse pointed to a woman in a worn white, wicker rocker in one corner of a stark white room. It was large enough to be a ballroom in a palace but, with broken blinds and bars on the outside of the windows, its' purpose was much more sinister.

"A word of caution, don't touch the doll. She'll fight you if she thinks you're gonna take it. Trust me you don't want to upset her. I'll check on those medical records you requested. I saw that the HIPPA forms come through earlier from your attorney." The nurse left.

As an after-thought Rose replied faintly, "Thank you." She found herself standing in front her birth mother. Overcome with a wave of unexpected emotions, Rose removed her sunglasses, scarf and gloves and knelt in front of the rocker. For a long-time she drank in those features so recognizable in herself.

What happened? What did you see that would make you want to leave reality?

Rose clutched the detectives' report in her hand. She'd read that Elizabeth Voss Harris had given birth to her only child, at twenty years of age. Rose's biological father served several tours in Vietnam and was released on a medical discharge but was considered a hero after single-handedly saving his entire platoon from certain death. He died, according to a single page, hand-written police report, of a gunshot wound to the chest. Rose's grandmother was the reportedly the shooter but she had died during the incident from a stab wound to her throat presumably from Rose's father. She struggled to find some commonality with the people she read about but it was more like reading the details of someone else's life, not hers.

The police officer who signed off on the report was James Boregard Hayden. Curious, Rose thought back to the parking garage at the hotel. *Sheriff Bo, James Boregard Hayden. are one in the same. Oh, dear God, what did he come to see me about?*

Rose stood and turned just as the nurse reappeared with an envelope. "Dr. Demazzo, sends his regrets. He can't meet with you today, after all. He has a patient in the emergency room at Grady Hospital but he asked me to give you this. It's the history of your mother's diagnosis and treatments."

Rose nodded an affirmative. Her hands trembled as she accepted the thick bundle. The nurse patted her on the shoulder and left.

Rose surrendered to the weakness in her knees and collapsed into a chair, silent, gazing at her mother face to face. Time had frozen the woman's features. Not a wrinkle blemished her porcelain skin. The resemblance between the two of them was uncanny. Their noses and cleft chin were identical. Looking at the woman's hands Rose saw her own in twenty years. Grey hair crept around the edges of Elizabeth's curly, auburn hair that highlighted violet in her pale blue eyes.

Rose reached for Elizabeth's hand. The instant she felt the soft warmth of flesh, Elizabeth let out a blood-curdling scream. Rose froze mouth agape.

Her mother clutched at the rag doll, rocking wildly, her eyes wide with fear, seeing some imagined terror. Rose watched as Elizabeth began to shake. A low groan rose up from a source of pain deep inside. It summoned a stabbing blackness in Rose's heart, tearing at her in a way she only wrote about in her books.

It took three nurses and an orderly to subdue Elizabeth long enough for her to receive an injection.

The nurse flew through the doorway toward Rose, shouting, "I told you not to touch that doll. It's the only thing that sets her off like that."

"I didn't", Rose retorted in her own defense, "I just, she…"

Rose and the nurse stood toe to toe, nose to nose, their words slapping each other's when…

"No more devil, Rose, no more devil, shhh, shhh, there now my dear sweet beautiful doll, it's all right. Daddy's gone a huntin'…" Elizabeth spoke.

Rose and the nurse turned. Elizabeth's voice, gentle and melodic, did not falter as she hummed the strange lullaby. The song struck a cord with Rose's eardrums. She melted in a heap on the floor beside Elizabeth's rocking chair. Rose began to hum in time with her mother. Out of tune at first but the words began to flow, "Hmm hmm, hmm, to catch a little rabbit skin to wrap his lil' buntin' in."

Elizabeth looked deep into Rose's eyes and for a moment there seemed to be clarity and recognition as she gently placed her fingertips under Rose's chin.

Rose reassured, "it's okay, Rose is safe." Elizabeth nodded.

She watched her mother slip away, back to the safety of the catatonia. Tears came to a burning crescendo in her eyes as Rose, now defenseless, laid her head on Elizabeth's knee.

Elizabeth stroked Rose's hair and hummed the rest of the lullaby while Rose wept.

Chapter Seven

The drive back to Atlanta was quiet. Rose felt thankful that DC had not been his usual, chatterbox self. The last thing she wanted was to have to put what happened into real words, she just wasn't ready for that.

Once back at her hotel and in the security of the blackout draperies Rose ordered up lunch but picked at the plate of shrimp, not convinced hunger could be responsible for the emptiness she felt inside.

She checked her flight online and changed the date of her return to an "open status". She just couldn't get on a flight. Seeing her mother answered some questions, but created more.

A knock at the door; Rose opened it to see the most beautiful array of red marble roses she'd ever seen, three dozen total. After tipping the bellhop she fumbled to find the little white envelope tucked deep inside the arrangement. The note, written in a script style with ink from a fountain pen or an inkwell, impressed her.

> *Your mother has missed you. As have I.*
> *Yours now and forever,*
> *Constantine*

Rose called the front desk, "Who sent these flowers to my room?"

The manager responded, "I'm sorry Ms. Bodin, no one saw who brought them in. They just appeared on the concierge desk with written instructions to deliver them to you at once."

After hanging up Rose phoned Jeff to see if there had been any stalker mail from a Constantine. Jeff always kept the nuts at bay. She never had to read the letters or e-mails.

Jeff knew right away, "Constantine? I can tell you that you get on average half a dozen marriage proposals from all kinds of nuts who call themselves Constantine. Why all the sudden interest? What's happened?"

"You know how I hate this kind of thing. How did this freak know where I was staying?"

"Everyone knows you're in Atlanta but did you consider that the vampire in your novels' is called Constantine? Every nut job in the country wants to be your Constantine. And, those are the nice ones. I turn all of the weird ones over to the police. And, yes, there are several who think they are the Vampire Constantine from your books."

"You've got to be joking? You seriously think some guy believes he is my character?" Rose's eye twitched as she recalled her dreams.

"I think they believe it to be true. But, of course, it's not possible, right?" Jeff snickered.

"Jeff, don't play with me. I just left an asylum where I witnessed my birth mother have an episode of some kind. Just tell me if there's really a nut job out there who thinks he is the Vampire Constantine?"

"Yes. I've gotten all kinds of weird stuff. But the police have copies of all the letters and emails. Your birth mother had an episode? I knew you were adopted but you didn't say a word about actually meeting your birth parents."

"Dr. G suggested I do some research to find out about my genetic and mental health history. So, I hired an investigator. Did a real good job, it took him less than two days to find her and all kinds of other shit."

"Dr. G suggested it? Huh? That figures, he has no idea what would happen if the press got wind of this. So, what'd you find out?"

"The short story, I had one messed up childhood. It's no wonder I made myself forget it."

"What about the press? How do you plan to comment? If they find out?"

"Tell me they don't know."

"Hell, Rose, I didn't know and I'm your publicist. But if they find out?"

"No comment."

"Do you want me to pick you up from the airport?"

"No. I changed my schedule. I left my return date open."

"Are you sure that's wise?"

"No, but I've got too many unanswered questions."

"Okay. I have to take this other call but I'll call you tomorrow and you can fill me in on the whole story, okay?"

Rose agreed and hung up. She pushed her chin into her chest, stretching the muscles in her neck. It felt good but what she really wanted was to curl up on the bed with the covers over her head. Instead, she pulled the laptop onto her lap and with a heavy sigh she began to spell check the last chapter.

I hate the way I've ended this chapter.

Rose scanned each word for errors and tried to come up with an alternate ending. Her eyes began to feel heavy and then a long and deep yawn brought tears to her eyes. Rose put her head down and drifted off to sleep.

A cold hand brushed across Rose's face startling, her. She jerked her body into an upright position and turned to see who or what touched her but she was alone. The closed draperies were now open. The thick pitch black of night stared back at her. Rose rubbed her eyes but it didn't help. Looking around the room, the furniture became fuzzy and out of focus.

I'm still asleep, I'm dreaming.

A noise came from the other room. Rose, trying to stand, tumbled from the bed. She lay on the floor, disoriented. *What the hell?*

Rose called out, "Who's there?"

Nothing, only the impenetrable darkness answered back.

Rose stood, the muscles in her legs quivering, she took a few steps away from the bed. Her legs gave way. With both arms extended she hit the door jam. Her grip didn't hold. She slid down the wall to the carpet.

"Dammit!" Rose shouted, as she lay prostrate.

Again, the icy hand, now joined by another, lifted her without effort. Rose, desperate to see who held her, blinked. Everything stayed blurry.

"What do you want?"

"You." A pure male voice resonated deep inside her body causing her to convulse. The arms were strong and his tone, commanding and unyielding.

"Am I drugged?"

"Not, really, just dazed," his laugh chided.

"Are you going to rape me or just kill me?" Rose tried to move. Unable to hold her head up it toppled against the man's solid icy, chest.

"No." He growled.

The floating sensation stopped. Rose reached out with one hand and felt the comforter of her bed. *Scream, dammit!* Her eyes searched unsuccessfully through the misty blur to see her captor. She opened her mouth to scream, but rallied a mere whimper.

"No, it will not help. You are not strong enough, yet."

Oh, God, help me.

A weight pressed hard over her chest but all she could see was the blur. She tried to rise and received a sharp pain in the right side of her neck that radiated through her. Arms refused to move tears welled then rolled down her temples to her hair.

The ringing in her ears became rhythmic, like a heartbeat!

Wake up! Please, wake up!

She opened her eyes and choked on the scream held captive in her throat.

Just inches above her, a man, levitated in a prone position. Except for a smear of crimson on his lips, his face took on the appearance of putty. The dark charcoal eyes widened as they stared deep into her soul. Yellow surrounded the black orbs, a thin circle of blood around the iris. Rose struggled but the weight on her chest increased.

What are you? What do you want with me?

The answer came as a deep voice echoing inside her head.

"I am Constantine. And soon you will have to die so you can live." He grinned and with his long, white finger lifted a tear away from the corner of her left eye and licked it. "I will have your blood and the completion of our union will solidify our eternity." He leaned in close and sniffed her. "You are delicious."

The ringing stopped the weight lifted as the scream inside her escaped. She sat up, sobbing, struggling to breathe. Her hand found her heart, *still beating.*

Her eyes darted from one corner of the room to the other. *I'm alive.* She rubbed her neck expecting to find blood but there wasn't any.

Rose, now able to focus, grabbed the phone and called the front desk, "Please!" She gasped, "Send security, there's someone in my room, 4122, hurry!"

Within moments the front door burst open and a male voice shouted, "Ms. Bodin, it's Jeremy, I'm coming in. Where are you?"

"Bedroom," she gasped, still too afraid to get off the bed.

A beam of light filtered through the room. Lights came to life as Jeremy entered wielding a black and yellow Maglite flashlight.

He circled the bed.

"The night guard's so old I left him to call the police. Are you all right, what happened?"

"There was a man and he…"

His eyes full of concern, "did he hurt you?"

Rose shook her head, pulled the blanket up to her nose and watched as Jeremy searched.

"There's no one here, now. I'll check the entire suite; you'll see it's okay."

Jeremy made his way into the living area. Rose got up and passed the open door just in time to see two police officers saunter into the living room. "Hey Jeremy, what's goin' on here?"

Rose quickly hid behind the bedroom door to listen.

In a hushed tone Jeremy replied, "Nothing, I think she had a nightmare. I can't find any evidence of an intruder."

She straightened her blouse and pushed the door shut with her foot. She rubbed away the traces of her tears and stood in the bright light of the bathroom, growing angrier by the moment.

Looking in the mirror she said, "Nightmare my ass!"

She splashed cold water on her face and rinsed her mouth.

Making her way back to the living area she was just in time to hear the officers joking, "Yeah and then the bastard had the quick wit to say 'these ain't my pants neither'." Everyone roared with laughter.

The policemen looked at Rose and then at their feet.

Placing a hand on her shoulder Jeremy asked, "Feeling better?"

"Yeah," she turned to the officers, "Thank you for coming so quickly. I'm sorry there's no one here for you to arrest."

Everyone, but Jeremy, nodded in agreement and made their way out. Rose closed the door, locked it and made a beeline to the bottles of red wine in the welcome basket.

"Would you like some?" Rose held a bottle of Red Zinfandel by the neck and shook it.

"Actually, I would. I'm off duty if you're sure you don't mind?"

"Are you kidding? I don't want to be alone right now. I'd appreciate your company."

Two bottles later Rose lay on the chaise sound asleep. Jeremy, in an upright position on the overstuffed chair, snored softly.

A shadow crossed over them. Constantine knelt next to Rose and licked at her pulsating jugular. Neither of them stirred as Constantine made his way out the window and into the pink haze of impending dawn.

Chapter Eight

A brisk knock on the door startled Rose from her slumber. Walking to the door she realized Jeremy had left and some-how she'd gotten into pajamas and her own bed.

"Who is it?" She looked through the peephole.

"Jeff." Answered the monotone male voice.

She muffled a potential squeal.

With the door wide open she flung herself into Jeff's arms, "Oh, my God, I can't believe it. What are you doing here?"

"Get me out of the hallway, I'll explain."

"Sorry, come in." Rose pulled him into the room by his sleeve. Jeff dropped his bag on the floor and took a seat on a barstool.

Jeff looked around at the suite, "Nice."

"You did good, thanks. So, what are you doing here?"

"I had to come. You were having so much fun."

"Liar. You came to check up on me. I know you, Jeffery. You can't pull that with me." Rose went into the mini fridge and retrieved a diet soda. "Want one?"

"No thanks. I want to hear it straight from the horses' mouth. So, what happened last night?"

"How did you —"

He raised his hand in a stop motion, "I left my number with the concierge the day I made your reservation. After the roses from "Constantine", Jeff made the parenthesis mark in the air, "I just didn't feel right about you being here alone. I had to come. Protect my interest." He chuckled, alone.

"You shouldn't have. I'm fine." *Great, I've been reduced to a freaking interest now.*

"I thought you'd say that. But you look like shit."

"Thanks, that's what a girl needs to hear first thing in the morning."

"It's three p.m.!" Jeff looked down at his watch.

"I didn't get any sleep until," she thought, "after the wine." She smiled thinking back at how gallant it was for Jeremy to have stayed. Seeing the mounting questions in Jeff's baby blue eyes Rose shifted the conversation, "You gonna bunk with me or did you get a room?"

Jeff wrapped his arms around her and gave her a big hug. He rubbed his palms up and down her back. Rose craved the affection and a familiar touch. But, when the tears began to sting her eyes, she pushed away from him.

"What the hell am I gonna do with you?" Rose forced a crooked smile to help her control the lump in her throat.

With one hand on his heart and the other in the air, "Don't ask what you can do for your publicist, ask what your publicist can do for you. I'm gonna help you settle this. Then, we go back to Dallas." He kissed her forehead. "My room wasn't ready, yet. The front desk will call here when it is. So, tell me all about this break down your birth mother had and the stranger who got into your room."

"It was horrible." Rose told Jeff everything. They laughed about the way everyone says Ma'am and the bumbling detective she'd hired. Room service brought the coffee, fruit and Danishes Rose ordered. The discussion turned serious when Jeff brought up the roses from Constantine.

"Did you see anyone suspicious at the book signing?"

"I did see one guy. See might be too strong of a word. I never got a good look at him, but something about his eyes, they were hypnotic."

"What about the intruder, could they be the same person?

"I'm not convinced it wasn't a dream. The guy actually floated above me.

Then he said some scary shit about, 'me having to die and our future together'. I think it could be just the stress of dealing with Elizabeth and my estate."

"Wow, sounds like a magician and a freak. I think we should go with dream until we have more evidence. Do you know what the estate entails, yet?"

"No." Rose took a long drink from the soda can, "I'm not sure I wanted to but after everything I've learned, I'm curious."

"Dr. Grant wanted to come but I talked him out of it."

"You spoke to him… about me? He told you what, exactly?"

"Nothing. I wanted to feel him out. I told him I was coming to see you and asked if I could do anything for you. Personally, I think he's hiding something."

"You mean like patient privilege."

"No. I think he's hiding something even more sinister, like his feelings toward you."

She rolled her eyes, "Don't be ridiculous. He is my doctor." Not sure how to react to the thought of Dr. Grant harboring feelings for her she fidgeted with her napkin.

"Like that's never happened in the history of psychiatry."

Rose stood, trying to change the subject, "I have an appointment tomorrow to meet with the executor of the estate, a Sonny James, the Fourth. I think I'm gonna have him put the house up for sale."

"Why? Are you sure there is a house?"

"I'm sure. My detective was thorough. I don't want any ties to this state. Elizabeth may never recover and if need be, I can move her to Texas. I just want to keep the press from going nuts with this so I can get out of this place. It gives me the willies and everything about it smells too damn sweet. It's nauseating."

The phone rang. Rose flinched.

"Easy, it's probably just the front desk about my room."

Rose answered the phone and confirmed that Jeff's room was ready. At the door they made plans to meet for dinner and hugged. Rose held on a few extra seconds, it felt good to hold a warm body.

Chapter Nine

Rose stepped out of the shower grabbed a towel and dashed for the buzzing phone next to the bed, "Hello!"

"Ms. Bodin, this is Mark Webber, with the Atlanta Journal Constitution. I hope I'm not intruding but your publicist said you were willing to do an interview. Is now a good time?"

Rose plopped down on the bed and sighed. She so wanted it to be Jeff, but work before well, work before everything.

"Now is fine."

"Great. I wanted to start by clarifying a few rumors. Are you a practicing vampire?"

"Exactly how does one go about practicing to be a vampire? Because aside from the fictional ones I write, there is no such thing as a vampire. They're legend, lore meant to frighten little kids into submission and nothing more. But to answer your question, no, I am not a practicing vampire."

"Who are you trying to convince? You have to admit your life reflects that you could be living out some of your own books."

"The fact is that I am photosensitive and have been since I was a little girl. I don't write vampire novels because I think I am a vampire. I write them because those are the books and stories I enjoyed so much during my sheltered childhood. If there were vampires, which there aren't, I certainly could understand how it feels to be isolated."

"Thanks for sharing that. I'm certain it had to be difficult. So, have you met with your birth mother?"

"How did you— this interview is over." Rose reached to hang up the phone when she heard the reporter yelling.

"No! No! Please don't hang up."

"Who told you about my mother?"

"So, it is true. I'll give you my source if you agree to let me have the exclusive on your time here in Atlanta, deal?"

"Deal, now, who told you about my mother?"

"Some lady, she wouldn't give her name, called me earlier today."

"Why call you?"

"The paper has been announcing your arrival and the book signing since you agreed to come to Atlanta and I'm the reporter for the literary section. I also do a monthly meet and greet if you're ever interested."

Rose cleared her throat, "all requests go through my publicist. What did the woman say?"

"She told me that your birth mother was in a local hospital. I wanted to scoop it because everyone knows you're adopted but with the privacy laws and stuff, well, it was feasible your birth parents could still be living here in Atlanta. It would be the story of the decade, finding the parents of the great vampire writer, Rose Bodin. But, to be honest the woman I spoke to gave me the creeps. At first, I really wasn't sure I could trust what she said. I'm not exactly Woodward or Bernstein. I am a humble, local guy who loves books. Just remember me when you're ready for your fans to know the truth. Okay? That's all I got, for now, can we finish the interview?"

"I guess, but no more personal questions and, yes, I will contact you if anything changes."

The rest of the interview went the way it was supposed to with the when and where of the next book, she's up for another award and there are always rumors of a movie.

"Hello." Rose answered her phone just moments after checking her make-up in the foyer mirror.

"Ms. Bodin, your car is here."

"Do you know where Jeff made reservations?"

"Yes, but I've been sworn to secrecy."

"Is it a nice place?"

"You could say that." He chuckled.

"So, I guess jeans are out of the question as the proper attire?"

"Not exactly?"

"Jeremy, where is he taking me for dinner? Come on, you can tell me."

"No ma'am, I can't. But jeans'll be fine. Trust me, you're gonna love it."

"Okay, I'll be down in a minute."

In 10 minutes Rose was nestled in the back of a town car with a single, red rose in the seat next to her. She lifted the thornless flower and put the firm pedals close to her nose and inhaled deeply. The fragrant aroma engulfed her senses and immediately put her at ease.

"Jeff you always know what I need."

The driver looked backed, "Ma'am?"

"Nothing, I was thinking out loud. Do you know where we are going?"

"I have instructions to deliver you to Grant Park."

"Is that a restaurant?"

"No, ma'am, it's a park." He shook his head.

"Oh, yeah, Grant Park." Rose felt a flush on her cheeks. *Why a park?*

It was already after midnight and the park appeared completely empty as the stealth black car crept silently along the narrow path toward a large gazebo. Something flickered in the distance as the car came to a stop. The driver opened the door and held out a hand to Rose. She took it and alighted from the car. The driver announced, "Ma'am, here," he extended his hand, "you almost forgot your flower."

"Thank you." Rose turned then took several steps toward the gazebo when the car turned a corner and disappeared. The darkness shattered as a sparkling light appeared. Jeff stood next to a white clothed picnic table and a large lit candle in the center.

He smiled and turned, "I believe your table is ready, madam."

"You are certifiable." She giggled and walked toward him.

"Well, I figured no one would be out this late and we would have a little privacy so we could enjoy a nice quiet dinner. I got your favorite, Sushi."

Rose could see the luscious bounty as she got closer. "Isn't this kinda dangerous?"

"Yes, but I'm not stupid." He nodded his head in the direction of a fountain and not far Rose could see several police officers wave at her. She waved and they enthusiastically waved more. "I hope you don't mind, I promised them signed copies of your next book." Jeff handed her a glass of champagne.

"Of course; I don't mind. I just have to finish the damn thing."

"Still bothered by the ending?" He lifted his own glass and touched the rim to hers lightly, "To midnight snacks."

"My favorite." Rose sipped the bubbly. "So, this seems awfully romantic."

"Don't be fooled, I haven't turned in my man card. I just wanted to let you see the more sensitive side of me. Besides, everyone in town knows you're here. You wouldn't be able to eat peacefully anywhere and eating in your suite isn't much fun."

"Very thoughtful, thank you. So, can we eat now, I'm starved."

Rose leaned back in her seat after devouring the last sashimi, "I'm stuffed and happy to have you here."

"I'm glad I came. We need to get this business done and get you home, safe. Have you met with the reporter, yet? It might stave off the other vultures if you can give them something."

"Yes, I did. It seems he has a female source and she told him that my mother is in a hospital here. Fortunately, he was most agreeable to accept my terms. And, I do want to try to give him the first interview when all this is said and done. Tomorrow, I have to see that attorney about the estate."

"Do you know what all is involved, is it property, stocks?"

"I don't know yet. He seems pretty hush-hush about it. He wants to meet me and go over a few things. Want to come with me?"

"I wouldn't miss it."

Chapter Ten

The attorney's office, a Georgian Style mansion, sat regally off Peachtree Road; a stoic surveyor to the history of Atlanta. The long driveway lined with Magnolia trees opened to a circle drive. In the center of the drive a plush fountain surrounded by wild rose bushes gurgled with flowing water. Rose gagged and swallowed hard as she exited the hotel's town car. She felt so out of place, "Please, wait here, we shouldn't be too long." The driver agreed.

Gas lanterns on either side of the blood red door flickered as the air grew heavy with humidity and the smell of Magnolia. Upon entering the great hall Rose and Jeff were led into an elaborate sitting room, offered iced tea and asked to wait by a most official looking butler.

Rose spoke first. "Do you think all the furniture is antique?"

"It looks like a bordello, if you ask me."

"And, how would you know?" Rose chuckled with her hand on her hip.

Jeff blushed.

The gargantuan room provided ample space for several different sitting areas. In the center of the room, the wooden floor, decorated with variations of painted constellations, glistened beneath several layers of wax.

"What do you think that means?" Jeff asked, as he pointed to a strange design in the center.

"I don't know. But it looks almost nasty, like angels and devils intertwined."

Rose rubbed her arms and shivered. "There's something about this place that gives me the hebbie-jeebies."

Jeff looked around anxiously, "it's old for one thing," then made his way to an overstuffed chair with a matching ottoman, "I think creepy is more to the point."

Rose walked over to one of three fireplace mantels. Examining an array of old photos. She stopped abruptly at one in particular. She picked up the gilded frame. The picture was of a man, a woman and a little girl. In the background she could see an older woman sitting on a porch swing. They looked like a happy family. After a few seconds she realized the little girl looked a lot like her. Her hands trembled and she abruptly put the frame back in its place.

". . . as long as he gets things done, who cares?"

Realizing she hadn't been listening to Jeff, she replied, "not me." Rose backed up keeping her eyes on the photo.

Doors opened.

Rose and Jeff turned to see an elderly black gentleman with hair almost as white as the gloves he wore enter and announce the attorney. "Master Sonny James the fourth, esquire."

"Rose, good glory woman you look exactly like Elizabeth." The man swaggered into the room with arms extended. He took both of her hands in his, "And, who is this?" He nodded toward Jeff.

"This is Jeffery Robinson, my publicist. Jeff this is Sonny James, the Fourth, Elizabeth's lawyer."

Sonny extended a hand, "Charmed. But I am your attorney as well, dear, and I am an attorney. Lawyer just sounds crass. I heard about your visit with Elizabeth." He made a tisk-tisk sound. "I hope you weren't too traumatized by her appearance." Aggrieved, he put the back of one hand on his forehead. "I try so hard to keep up with her hair and clothing. But, alas, it's near impossible. Here," he motioned, "have a seat so we can get reacquainted."

Rose wasn't sure if she should sit on the delicate furniture. The already thread bare fabric looked as if it would melt at the slightest hint of a pull. She avoided the small wooden chairs for fear of injury to herself.

"That's better." Sonny wriggled onto the seat next to her.

"I came to see what my options are on the estate."

Sonny tilted his head and stitched his arched eyebrows, "Options? Rose, yours is one of the oldest homes in Atlanta. The entire neighborhood is in danger from young professionals building silly Mcmansions. You can't be thinking of selling." Sonny leaned in toward her.

"Yes, I am." Dodging Sonny's stare Rose looked at Jeff.

Jeff leaned in to give his opinion but Rose stopped him with a quick shake of her head.

"You've not even seen the house! How can you consider selling?" Sonny began fanning himself and rolling his eyes in disgust.

"I don't know anything about my…family. I don't want to be tied down in a bunch of legal mumbo-jumbo over some estate."

"Legal mumbo-jumbo!" Sonny's eyes became lasers his face contorted and reddened, "That house, the entire estate is your legacy." He leaned within inches of her face, "I don't believe Elizabeth or Grannie would approve of your selling."

"Grannie? If you're referring to my grandmother, she is dead and I can only assume that she left the house to Elizabeth and well, she's still alive, right? So something has you contacting me about all this now. And as long as it's up to me, I will do as I see fit. Besides you said it yourself, you're my attorney too."

"She'd turn over in her grave if she heard you talk like this. It's just not proper." He sat back, flat against the cushions, legs crossed tight and one hand on his knee, "I remember when you referred to the rose garden as your Eden, or have you forgotten that too?"

"Forgotten that too?" Rose turned red with anger and perched herself on the edge of the seat. "I have no memory of my childhood before I was adopted! It's not a matter of what I've forgotten. But, how is it you know so much? You're just an attorney, right?"

Sonny took a deep raggedy breath. "I suppose I can put the house on the market. But," he shook his finger at Rose, "I refuse until you've been there. I thought by now your memory would have returned."

Rose shook her finger at him, "You're the one with all the answers, you and your father. What can you tell me about my family?"

"It's not polite to discuss ones' dirty laundry in public." Sonny placed his finger over his lips in a hush motion and uncrossed his legs.

"What public? It's my family." Looking at Jeff, "Him? He's okay. You can say anything in front of him."

"I'm not at liberty to discuss what no one knows for sure. There are rumors. Even one that you killed them in a fit of jealousy."

Rose jumped up. "Bullshit! I was what 5 or 6?! You obviously know more than you're telling. And, there is a police report that in no way points to me as the assailant. And, as long as the house is in trust to me or whatever, you have an obligation to me."

"Fine! But what I know isn't much. Your grandfather died in 1960, your grandmother made some very wise stock moves with the retirement he left her. Rumor is that she had a fortune before she married him. But, for some odd reason they chose to live rather spend thrift lifestyles. You are set for life, sweetie." Sonny stood glancing out the window at the gray pink light of dusk. He leaned over and glared at her, "No one knows what happened that night, except you."

"I can't believe this. If you want me to do anything with that house you need to come up with better answers than that." Rose motioned for Jeff to follow, she turned, spied the photo on the mantle.

"By the way, when was that picture taken?" She pointed to the framed family portrait. Mr. James straightened his magenta tie as he sauntered toward the mantel.

He took a business card and a set of keys from his jacket pocket, "Ms. Bodin, you need to go to the house. And take the sheriff you look so much like Elizabeth you could scare the bejeebers out of neighbors. Here's the address and the keys. Call me when you've had a change of heart."

Rose snatched them from his hand noticing beads of sweat collecting on his forehead and upper lip.

He relieved the frame of the photo, handed it to Rose, "You can have it."

"Damn it, I want to know when the picture was taken!" The photo shook in her hand.

"It was taken the same day you lost your memory and your family. That's all I know, if you'll excuse me." He pulled a tasseled cord by the fireplace. Within seconds the butler reappeared.

"Charles, please see that our guests find their way out. I'll be in touch, Ms. Bodin. Good-bye." Sonny turned and disappeared through a paneled door. There was nothing left to say or anyone to say it to so they followed the obedient butler out the front door. Their driver waited in the circle drive.

"What the hell just happened? I've never seen you so aggressive and willing to attack." Jeff took Rose by the shoulders, squaring her up. "It's obvious he's nervous about something. But I've never seen you so emotionally charged. He really got to you." Jeff put his arms around Rose and held her tight. The butler cleared his throat as he opened the door to go back inside. Rose looked up and through a top window she saw curtains relax back into place.

"It's this place, there's just something about it. I don't care what his problem is, I'm gonna look at the house and then he has to sell it."

"Whatever you say, you're the boss, applesauce."

"Damn straight!" Rose looked back at Jeff. He made the funny face, the one that always makes her laugh. "I'm so glad you're here."

"Me too." Jeff opened the car door and gave instructions to the driver.

Once inside and on their way, Jeff put his arm around Rose, she leaned into him. *God, he smells nice.*

Chapter Eleven

ntering her room, Rose noticed the light on the phone next to her sofa blinking. She called the automated voice mail system while Jeff tinkered with the ice bucket.

Hanging up the phone Rose turned to Jeff. "Well, that does it, Sonny called the sheriff."

"Why?"

"The sheriff left me a message saying he wants to meet at the house tomorrow. I guess Mr. James didn't think I'd do it."

"That's great!"

Rose's stomach knotted at the thought of seeing the house although she wasn't sure why, she had no memory of it or her family. Maybe the thought that they all died there, maybe, but all this made her head ache.

Jeff held up a pamphlet and shook it. "Let's take in some sights. How about 'Underground Atlanta'?"

"So long as I can get a drink."

Jeff handed her a sheet of paper, "Here, I printed out directions to the house."

Rose folded the map and stuffed it in her purse. On the way out the door she felt a chill on the nape of her neck. Looking back, the room was empty but there was something, something that made it feel occupied and sinister. Rose shook it off.

"What kind of surprise?" Rose kept her eyes shut tight as Jeff guided her through the lobby.

"Don't worry, you'll love it."

"I'd better, I feel like an idiot."

"Open." Jeff removed his hands.

A black Lexus with tinted windows sat regally in the driveway. It made her eyes swell with tears. Rose let out the tiniest of squeals, wrapped her arms around Jeff's neck. "How'd you find it?"

"You can rent anything you just have to know someone." Jeff winked and nodded toward Jeremy standing behind the valet stand. Rose grabbed the key from Jeff and jumped into the driver's seat.

"Fasten your seat belt!" She turned the key and the motor purred to life.

They were off in a flash. They had an hour to meet the sheriff at the house so they took the scenic route through downtown.

Rose maneuvered the car through traffic with ease. As soon as they hit the freeway Jeff began to look around inside the car.

"What are you looking for?"

"The map I printed last night, I thought I had it."

"It's still in my purse."

"And, where's that?"

Rose giggled and held up her little travel purse, "My other purse, at the hotel."

"Great." Jeff rolled his eyes.

Rose exited Ralph Abernathy Rd. and brought the car to a screeching halt in front of a small mom & pop grocery store.

"We can get directions here. It looks like a friendly place and I have a feeling we're close."

Jeff exited the car in a rush but Rose, quick as ever, beat him to the door. A rusty old, bell attached to the front door, announced their arrival. Several shoppers turned to see who'd entered but quickly went about their own business. Jeff and Rose made it to the back of the store where several older gentlemen sat at a table drinking soda while playing dominos. In turn each man looked up. Their mouths agape, they stared motionless. Rose looked up at Jeff to gauge his reaction.

"Do you think they recognize me from my books?"

"I doubt it. These geezers don't look like they've read much." Jeff took Rose's hand in his.

One of the men jumped to attention, knocked over the plastic chair as he shouted, "Ruby! You better get out here."

A woman's voice echoed from the back, "What's a matter Bufford, run outta pennies…?"

A tall, robust woman appeared from behind a draped doorway, she took stock of the men but fixed her eyes on Rose. Ruby let out a quick and short grasp, dropped the box she held and clutched her heart.

"Good God Oh Mighty! 'Lizabeth, that cain't be you."

Rose stepped toward the woman with her hand extended, "Hi, I'm Rose Bodin. I use to live around here."

"'Lizabeth's Rose?" The woman shook her head without acknowledging Rose's extended hand.

"Yes, ma'am." *Did I just say ma'am?*

"Child, you're the spitting image o' your mamma. Sorry about the men here, they don't got no manners." The woman slapped the bald-head of the man sitting nearest to her. He jumped from his chair and offered it to Rose. She respectfully declined.

"I just need directions to Gordon Place."

"You're not but two blocks from there." One man snorted.

"Why'd you come?" Another asked.

"I came to see the house but I left my map at the hotel. My cell service is spotty."

"Seems to me you knew exactly where you's a goin', to end up here." Ruby retrieved her box and placed it on a counter. "You and your grandma use to walk to this store to get you Fig Newtons. You'd eat 'em by the dozen."

Sensing Rose's distress, Jeff put his hand on her shoulder. She took a deep breath.

She gave Jeff her biggest smile then turned to the woman. "And, you are?"

"I'm Ruby Johnston. I was your neighbor, 'fore . . ." She hung her head.

"You seem to have known my family well?"

"My mother was your grandmother's best friend. I knew your mamma, too. I was a few years older than her, though." The woman brushed back a salt and pepper clump o' hair that had made its' way to her forehead. "I was married with two young 'uns o' my own by the time you was born. When I came to visit, we'd all sit on the porch in that swing your Grandaddy built. We'd talk and sip sweet tea for hours. You loved to stand on the stoop. You'd sing to anyone who'd listen, Loretta Lynn songs mostly but a hymn or two when your Grannie asked for one. It was the cutest thing. Weren't scared to talk to strangers." Ruby choked back a tear and pulled a white hanky from her apron pocket to dab her eyes. "It was the most horrible thing to happen in this neighborhood."

Rose swallowed hard, "What happened?"

Ruby folded her arms and cocked her head to one side, "Don't you know?"

"No."

The bald man spoke out, "Everyone thought you did it."

The dead silence abruptly broke when the bell on the door rang out as someone entered the store. Everyone looked up but no one could see the person responsible. Rose shook as an all too familiar cold chill greeted nape of her neck. The room became fuzzy. People seemed to be talking but she couldn't make-out what they were saying. Her head began to spin and her chest felt heavy. Rebekah's strange perfume, that had made her ill at the café, flitted through her sinuses. She covered her mouth to prevent herself from gagging. Just when she thought she could take no more a firm hand took hold of her left shoulder. Everything wounded back into gear like a reel to reel abruptly taken off slow motion. A moan escaped her covered mouth.

Embarrassment flooded her cheeks with color as she looked up to see Sheriff Bo standing beside her.

"You were late. I came to get a soda. I see you've met Ruby and the gang."

Rose swallowed hard trying to get rid of the sweet, pungent odor lingering in her throat.

The sheriff looked at Ruby, "Everyone has their own opinion of what happened. But it's still a private family matter, right Ruby?"

"Right, Sheriff." Ruby turned toward the back whispering under her breath as she exited.

"Rose, let's go so we can talk to the Sheriff . . ." Jeff looked around at the inquisitive eyes, ". . . in private." He tugged at her elbow until she followed. The three walked out.

In the parking lot the sheriff was first to speak, "Follow me, it's only a block or two and no more detours."

Jeff started the car and headed out into traffic.

"Dr. G told me all my memories are stored in my brain. I already have all the answers. But I threw away the password. Maybe just being here is slowly opening the vault and that's why I got here without the map. If so, that's part of what terrifies me, what I may already know but won't see coming."

Chapter Twelve

She quickly kissed Jeff on the cheek and got out of the car. She took a deep breath, lifted her eyes to face the house. The house was not imposing. A gush of relief surprised her. She realized the house wasn't a horrible boogieman waiting to steal all her hopes and dreams. It was just a house and an old one at that. The sidewalk she stepped onto bulged from the roots of a giant oak tree. Rose looked down the tree-lined street at the rest of the houses. Without restraint Rose began to laugh. She laughed until her eyes were wet with tears. The two men stood by not sure what to make of her unusual response.

"I'm sorry. I guess I just built this thing up into some sort a haunted house that was gonna reach out and eat me the moment it saw me." She wiped her eyes and headed up the walk.

She stopped at the front door and turned back to the sheriff, "I'm not gonna find any bodies, am I sheriff?"

The Sheriff approached. Placing one boot on the bottom step he leaned forward. He took off his sunglasses, hung them on the pocket of his shirt and with a serious tone, "This was my first homicide. I've never seen anything like it since. I pray I never do. I realize this is gonna be hard for you but try not to make light of something so tragic just 'cause you don't remember it." Rose retrieved the key from her pants pocket.

Looking square into the eyes of the sheriff, "You're right." She pointed her finger, "You were there and you saw. But, let me assure you, it was only the tip of the iceberg. What happened before you arrived had to be so horrible it made me want to forget my entire family and it sent my mother to an asylum, quite possibly for the rest of her life. So, if I tend to break the spell with a bad sense of humor, I damn well earned it." Rose sniffed back fury laced tears, refusing to succumb to the emotional torrent. The momentary silence announced a truce.

Rose turned the key and opened the door.

The bright and cheerful living room shined as tiny streams of sunlight poured in from a broad picture window on the Eastside. The overstuffed furniture, though worn and dated, looked inviting. Rose prayed for a flicker of recognition, but nothing.

The marble fireplace glistened. Flowers overflowed from the hearth. Photos placed on the mantel sparkled with life.

Rose walked to the center of the room. Her left hand trembled so it got stuffed into her pocket. Emotions began to swell in her chest. *Why?*

A picture of a little girl hung by a pink velvet ribbon. Another photo, a couple dressed in their wedding finery, posed happily on a step in a garden. Their faces glowed with the unmistakable warmth of true love. Those moments, frozen in time, so tender and precious, caused Rose to turn away.

Regret washed over her forcing tears to well and a knot to form in her throat. She gasped for the breath she'd forgotten about.

"I need to do this." Rose announced.

Rose moved toward a wall. She ran her finger down the molding then gently parted the door panels.

Jeff crooked his head to one side, "How'd you know that was a door?"

Rose shrugged as a tingling went up and down her spine, "Just did."

On the other side of the paneled doors the dining room walls were amassed with framed portraits of all shapes and sizes. Strangers stared at her from their perches.

At the head of a dining table, set for eight, a vase filled with red roses emitted enough perfume to fill the room.

On a glass shelf inside the massive china cabinet a silver rattle wrapped with a pink ribbon sat untarnished. On the ribbon, gold embossed numbers, 06-05-65, 7 lbs. 8oz. 19", born 2:11 p.m., Agnes Rose Harris. Rose felt warm as her cheeks flushed. She walked past the buffet table and back to the paneled door.

Looking to her left, Rose could see a door at the end of a long hallway. Sunlight forced its way through every available crack around the molding. Her heart raced.

Unable to control her legs, Rose walked through the house and directly to the backyard.

The ancient Magnolia stood, defiant and proud, its' limbs spanned half the distance to the fence. Unable to turn away, Rose walked steadily toward the tree. She reached for a bloom the wind snatched it from her grasp. The willing branches parted to reveal a large open space where no grass grew. Rose waited for breath as a musty stank invaded her airway.

The cold and molded air invaded every pore of Rose's skin. She shivered. Her heart pounded. A bead of sweat dropped from her nose to the dry unforgiving dirt. The limbs snapped shut. Darkness. Off balance, Rose stumbled.

The grossly sweet scent of the magnolia blossoms oozed down the back of Rose's throat causing her to swallow hard. Unable to complete the act she gagged and coughed.

Rose commanded her feet to move but they rebelled. She tried to cry out but choked. Looking down the ground spun around her feet. Arms outstretched, Rose reached for something, anything, to stop the motion.

Ice touched her hand. She tried to pull away but the coldness had a grip on her. It tightened around her wrist. Her body fell forward and into the arms of Constantine.

His chest hard and solid lacked the warmth of human skin. Depraved eyes leered down on her. She wanted to scream but could only stare and tremble in the grasp of a monster.

A voice resonated close to her ear, "Want to play?"

A flash of bright light then . . .

Rose opened her eyes, dizzy and nauseated. Everything stopped. She could hear people shuffling about. Whispers floated and then echoed back to her ears. She moaned. A cold cloth placed on her forehead made her shiver. She looked up to see the angelic face of a man-child. He spoke. His voice gentle but that of a man.

"Feel better?" He leaned in close to her, blinking.

"I think so. Who are you?" Rose pulled up to a near sitting position.

"I'm Dwayne. You're Rose." He pointed his finger at her nose.

The sheriff entered from the dining room holding a small jelly glass brimming with water, "This oughta help."

"You were out that door so fast and within a minute we found you all spaced out. What the hell happened Rose?" Jeff reached out his hand but Rose dismissed it by reaching for the glass of water.

As the sheriff handed her the glass he nodded toward Jeff, "Yeah, that's what we were hoping you can tell us."

After several seconds Rose turned to Jeff, "Did you see him?"

Confused Jeff asked, "Who?"

"The man in the tree!" Rose's voice became several octaves higher than normal.

"No. I heard you cry out and when I got there you had fainted. I picked you up and carried you in here."

"There was someone there. A man. I think it was the same one who broke into my room."

The sheriff turned to Dwayne, "Dwayne were you in the tree?"

Dwayne began to bite his nails and rock back and forth on his heels.

"It's okay, you're not in any trouble. We just need to know if it was you." Jeff's voice though calm did nothing to defuse Dwaynes' anxiety.

The young man pointed to Rose. "She knows. Her boogie man."

Stunned, Rose's mouth dropped open. Silence reigned while each person digested the words.

The sheriff cleared his throat. "Dwayne there's no such thing as a boogie man."

Agitated, Dwayne began to pace, "Her boogie man. Her boogie man." He repeated over and over.

Rose stood, locked eyes with Dwayne, "Have you seen my boogie man?"

"Yeah."

"What does he look like?"

"Black hair. Mean eyes. Smells bad." Dwayne pinched his nose.

"Have you talked to him?"

"Kinda. He said Rose come home. I got roses. You like roses."

A shudder of fear reverberated through Rose's entire body. "The roses in the dining room?" *He's real!*

She wrapped her arms around Dwayne. He sucked in a hiccup breath, "Rose home."

"Yes, Dwayne, I'm home. I'll take care of the boogie man."

"Make him go away?" Dwaynes' sad sweet eyes added to the plea.

"I feel like I've stepped into a classic horror film. Without the script." Rose stroked Dwaynes' chubby cheek.

"Happy." Dwayne clapped his hands, "Rose home." He ran out the front door letting the screen door slam shut.

The sheriff shook his head, "I think it's time you hear what I saw and maybe you'll be able to fill in some of the blanks."

"I want to destroy the shroud over my memories. I want to remember. But there's this blackness I can't get through." The Sheriff patted her on the knee and sat back on the sofa. He took a deep breath and began his journey to the past.

"When I heard the call on the radio, shots fired, I recognized the address. We had been out here a couple times before on domestic disturbances. Your daddy had, what we called then, shellshock. It's the horrors of war that sometimes come home with a vet. Nam got to a lot of guys. Your father was one of the last to come home. I was close so I responded. I was excited 'cause I would be the first officer on the scene. I was just a deputy then, still wet behind the ears, but anxious. Once on the porch I expected to hear arguing, as with most domestic disputes, but there wasn't so much as a cricket. I readied my service revolver and opened the screen door." He rubbed his eyes as the image of what he'd seen next came into focus.

"The first thing to hit me was the metallic odor of blood. The residue from a gun blast still hung in the air. It mixed with the blood in an eerie way and, the blood, so much blood. I saw your daddy, Charles lying face down his feet still on the cushion of a chair." He pointed to the now empty corner, paused, remembered.

"From the waist up he was on top of your grandmothers' body. His hand still clutched the knife protruding from her throat. I realized it was his bayonet by the muzzle ring. Training must've took over 'cause you don't get prepared for that kinda scene. I checked for pulses, there weren't any. That's when I saw you crouching between the arm of the chair and the sofa. You were drenched in blood, your eyes blank. Then, I heard your mother. She cried out, holding a rag doll. She rocked back and forth in the corner by the fireplace. She too was splattered in blood although I saw no wounds." He paused.

Rose handed him the glass of water. He drank it down in one gulp.

"We can stop." Rose took the glass and placed it on the floor by her foot.

"No. I need to get this out. I've held it in far too long." He adjusted his position and continued, "I asked if you were hurt. You just stared at me with those empty eyes. I checked your hands and face for wounds."

Rose interrupted, "Was I hurt?"

He shook his head, "Nothing physically that I could see, I picked you up, carried you out of the house. Dwayne and his mother came from next door to see what the fuss was about. She'd called in when she heard the gun shot. I handed you off to her. By that time, the Sheriff, backup officers and ambulances took over the scene." He paused, wiped beads of sweat off his forehead before he continued.

"The coroner determined your grandmother killed your daddy with a single shotgun blast to the chest. I figured your mom saw it up close because of the splatter on her face and neck. He stabbed your grandmother with his bayonet likely as he charged over the chair. We knew Charles had been released from his final tour of Vietnam on a medical discharge. We could only speculate what his mental condition must've been. Your mother witnessed the event but she's not been able to tell us what sparked such a violent confrontation. You went into the custody of the state until the family attorney, Sonny James took you in. It didn't take long for Mr. James to get custodial rights to have you put up for adoption. You know the rest."

Rose got up and walked out the front door. Jeff followed. They sat in the swing unable to put two words together. Jeff took Rose's hand. Caressing it, he brought it to his lips. The warmth the softness against her skin weakened her defenses. She wanted to let go.

She laid her head in the crook of his shoulder. Jeff brought his arms around her and squeezed tight. Unable to think of a reason to bolt Rose gave herself over to the safety of Jeff's embrace. As she relaxed her body her mind followed allowing tears to swell to an uncontainable crescendo.

Rose cried torrents. Her body shook with the release of emotions she'd governed for so long. The regret over what she'd lost was evident and overwhelming. She clawed at her memory, desperate to remember that night or any night from her childhood. Still, the veil remained taunting her.

The sky turned pinkish lavender by the time Jeff spoke, "We should get back. You haven't eaten today."

"I'm not hungry. I'm exhausted."

"I know, but you need to keep up your strength. Let me —" With his hand under her chin he lifted her face to his and leaned in. Rose quivered at the first whisper of his lips on hers. She wanted to crawl inside him.

After several indulgent embraces she pulled away, "I don't want pitty."

"What pitty, you're buying dinner." Jeff chuckled.

Rose went back into the house to say goodbye to the sheriff.

He wiped his eyes with defeated hands and stood there alone in the dark, keys in his hand. "I turned off the lights and locked up. Dwayne takes care of the place he keeps a set of keys." He lifted his hand to show her the keys. "I wish I…"

"You did all you could, the rest is up to me. Whoever did this to me and to my family will pay for what they've done. I will get my memories back, eventually. Thank you, Sheriff." She reached out to hug him. He advanced with open arms.

The embrace was familiar and comforting. Her heart ached. She wanted to erase the horrifying visions of that night from his memory even though she desperately wanted to remember them.

Chapter Thirteen

It took several seconds for her to recognize her hotel room. She rubbed her eyes and tried to focus through the sleepy haze.

"I thought you were gonna sleep all day."

Rose turned toward the voice. "Jeff!"

He sat on the chaise. "Who were you expecting?"

"The way things have been going, Boris Karloff, maybe. What time is it?"

He offered her a cup of coffee. Rose took the steamy drink.

"After four."

Rose sipped the hot liquid and reveled in its' warmth. "Thanks, it's good."

Jeff nodded then sat on the bed next to Rose. "Bad dreams?"

"Of course, but I can't remember them, why?" She lifted a finger, tapped her temple.

"You were breathing kinda odd in your sleep."

"Odd?"

"It was like panting, short quick breaths."

"I don't remember how I was breathing but I do remember you ordering room service and running a bath while I ate."

"You didn't make it to the bath. You fell asleep before the tub filled up."

Silence consumed the inches between them. Awkwardness had never been there before and Rose hated feeling vulnerable. Remembering the kiss she felt she had to say something.

Her head down, eyes on the swirl of cream in the coffee, "I really liked the kiss. I just hadn't thought of us like that before."

"There's time for that. Right now, you need to get your memory back so you can get away from this place." He leaned over, kissed her forehead.

Rose, conscious of her appearance, brushed back her untamed hair, a nervous grin bent the corners of her mouth "I must look a mess." She put the coffee on the nightstand and headed into the bathroom to assess the damage. She turned on the shower and called out, "I'll just be a minute."

"Take your time. I'll be here."

Rose hummed as she combed through wet tangles. Felling completely refreshed she got dressed and exited the bathroom. In the living room Jeff stood with his back to her. He was on the phone. Rose cleared her throat. Jeff rounded to face her. His expression kicked her in the gut. She held her breath, terrified of what was being said on the other end.

"What?" Rose clenched her fist controlling the urge to grab the phone.

"I'll have her there as soon as possible." Jeff hung up the phone his hands now gripped her upper arms. Rose braced herself. *This is gonna be bad.*

"It's your mother."

"What's happened?" Rose fought tears.

"She's had an accident."

"Which mother?"

"Sorry, Elizabeth, she's in the ICU. They want you there right away."

The elevator door opened to the bustle of the 4th floor ICU at Grady Memorial Hospital. Elizabeth's physician, Dr. Demazzo, stood two feet away in bloody scrubs with a stethoscope dangling from around his neck barking orders to a bevy of nurses and technicians. His salt and pepper hair disheveled and his beard several days overgrown.

"Doctor Demazzo." Rose paused. He nodded. She continued, "How's my mother?"

He motioned for them to follow, "She's in ICU 8 I'll go with you so we can talk."

"What happened?" Rose struggled to keep up with the doctors' long strides.

"Well, Miss Bodin."

"Please, call me Rose."

They entered the room. Rose took a step back. The metallic odor of blood rattled the veil of secrecy in the dark recesses of her mind. A bright light, as the glimpse of a memory, flashed. People yelling, voices all at once, the flash of gunfire, another scream and then it disappeared. She shook her head and swallowed hard then went to Elizabeth.

Dr. Demazzo continued, "The night nurse heard a scream. She found Elizabeth on the floor clawing at her throat. Upon examination I found jagged tears all the way to her jugular. I did what I could to repair the damage but she's suffered substantial blood loss. She received several pints of blood in the OR but she may need more. Do you know your blood type?"

Rose looked confused, "No. Why?"

"Your mother has an O negative blood type and can only receive the same. The nurse will need to get a blood sample to cross and type."

"Of course." Rose rolled up her sleeve.

A nurse waiting by the door motioned, "No, hon, I just need to do a finger prick."

Rose winced simultaneously with the snap of the spring-loaded pen needle. Blood filled the tiny glass tube immediately. "Dr., will she recover?"

He tilted his head. "She's in critical but stable condition, for now. I won't sugar coat this, that could change at any moment." He opened the door to leave then turned, "I've done all I can for the time being. I'll be back to check on her after rounds."

The nurse had what she needed and turned to walk out the door when Jeff touched her on the arm, "where can I get some coffee?"

"You can follow me it's on the way to the lab."

Rose never heard them leave. She leaned over the bed and whispered into Elizabeth's ear, "I'm here, Mom."

After several empty moments Rose kissed her mom's forehead and suddenly felt tired. She made her way to the leather recliner by the window. Her body ached with tension. She needed to sit. Habit caused her to run her fingers through her hair. She realized it was still damp and she wasn't wearing make-up. "God I must look awful." She put her head back against the headrest of the chair.

Hums, ticks and beeps from the monitors and the oxygen machine lulled Rose into a deep state of relaxation.

Without warning the room turned frigid. Rose shivered and opened her eyes.

She tried to stand but a force weighted her deep into the cushion.

An icy voice, "I will destroy anyone who gets in my way."

She looked around the room. The air began to thicken. Silence. A white haze appeared over the bed. The thin mist whirled and grew upward over the prostrate body on the bed. Features began to take shape. The room lightened. A warm glow radiated from the near translucent figure. The iciness she had felt dissipated leaving only the warm feeling of being held in loving arms.

In seconds the mass became the angelic and youthful Elizabeth. She smiled, extended her arms.

Rose's face went flush from the warmth.

Elizabeth spoke, "Rose, my dear sweet beautiful doll. Be strong. You can defeat him. I love you. I will be with you, always."

The glow dissipated. The room came alive with alarms and buzzers. A voice on the intercom commanded, "Code blue, ICU 8 Code blue, ICU 8, STAT!" Doctors and nurses exploded into the room. A ballet of medical procedures went into production.

After what felt like hours the doctor looked up with the stethoscope still pressed against Elizabeth's chest. Everything went still when the doctor pronounced, "9:22 p.m."

Chapter Fourteen

ose swung both feet to the pavement and dragged herself, with the helping hand of the driver, from the black limousine. *This was not what I came to Atlanta for, to bury my mother.* The last words her mother had spoken to her echoed, 'You can defeat him.'

She adjusted her long black skirt, took a deep breath and made her way towards the mass of people gathered around a minister. She felt the weight of the world on her chest. Another deep exhalation did little to relieve the pressure. *What did her mother know of the man seemingly haunting her?* Even the sun's late afternoon rays could not penetrate the coldness gathering around the edges of Rose's heart. Nor could they pass through the long sleeves and gloves and the hat with a veil. *This is not fair, dammit, I'm a stranger here and I must look like a freak to these people.*

She approached the group of mourners. Each person took turns sharing their grief through tear filled eyes and regretful glances. Thoughts raced. *How can so many remember Elizabeth? She's been confined for so many years. All these flowers will have to be dealt with. Where can I send them? What do I say to these sad people? How can I help them? I shouldn't be here, this isn't right. This is so wrong. I want to go home.*

The nurse, who just days before had been put out by Rose's presence, smiled.

"Your mother was loved by everyone who looked after her. Unfortunately, no one else from the hospital could be here. Think of me as their representative. We will miss her." The once imposing caregiver's lips trembled as she spoke. The nurse turned to catch her tears in a lace hanky she'd retrieved from her sleeve.

The minister opened his bible and cleared his throat:

"Proverbs says that a virtuous woman's price is higher than rubies. That she will do good and not evil all the days of her life. Her children will arise and call her blessed and her husband will praise her."

Sniffles and short bursts of sobs forced Rose's own sense of loss up into her throat. *How can I mourn a woman I don't remember? I feel loss but for what? Elizabeth had so many friends. She had to have been special. God, why now?*

"The final-line of the verse states, 'Give her the fruit of her hands; and let her own works praise her in the gates.' Elizabeth, we bow our heads in prayer that you have received the praise and final peace you so richly deserve."

Rose visualized the apparition that hovered over Elizabeth's dying body. The warmth and peace that resonated from the ghostly image was undeniably Elizabeth.

Oh God, I'm just beginning to know this woman and I miss her.

The casket lowered inch by inch until Rose could no longer see the blanket of red roses that covered the dark wood lid. She began to count the number of elaborate arrangements surrounding her. It was amazing how many people came together to make all of the arrangements for the funeral.

Her nose caught a whiff of Magnolia. The back of her throat tightened. Sadness turned to fear as each pore tingled to attention. The coolness of the breeze now stung her cheeks with an iciness that sent shivers through her.

I know you're here. I feel you.

Rose examined every face that passed. She heard her name but could not find the source. Her breath became shallow her gloved hands rung with anticipation.

The pastor approached his hands extended, "Rose. I'm so sorry for your loss." He placed her gloved hands in his. The warmth of his hands melted through the stretchy fabric of her gloves and caused all fear to dissipate as fast as it had materialized. "Your mother was a valued member of this community. We will surely miss her. If there's anything I can do —"

From behind a mausoleum a man ran towards them shouting, "Miss Bodin, Miss Bodin. How do you feel about losing your mother?"

Rose's first thought; *That's strange, a reporter at a funeral.*

Just behind him several more paparazzi bobbed and weaved past tombstones. Pastor James called out, "Rose?"

Me, they're here for me! Rose looked for the fastest exit when she spied Jeff running toward her.

"How the hell did they find me?" She shouted in mid stride. Rose stopped, turned back to the pastor, "Sorry!"

"That's okay. You go. I'll fend them off as long as I can."

Jeff grabbed her arm and guided her toward the idling car. They jumped in and Jeff hit the gas. Rose looked back to see the pastor waving a Bible high above his head while chasing a cameraman.

Rose laughed nervously, "Great. Now I have the clergy defending me with the word of God."

She turned her attention to Jeff. "How did the press find out?"

"I got wind of it as I was getting dressed for the funeral. I am sorry, that's why I was so late, I held them off as long as I could. One of my guys in New York called me to see if the story was true. I told him I couldn't comment but he said it didn't matter because there were several reporters on their way to the cemetery. I parked the car as close as I could. Are you okay? You look kinda spooky all in black."

"I'm fine but I think I know how they found out. That one reporter for the Constitution, he said that someone had tipped him off to me looking for my mother."

"Deaths are a public record and so are a lot of other things, like filing of Probates and wills. And trust me there are goons who watch the courthouse for a famous name to pop up. From that point they just call funeral homes until they find the right one. It's not a secret that you're here. Your mother was a popular lady and the pastor said her estate has been very generous to the community."

"Where are we going?"

"Your attorney's office."

"Why?"

"He wants to meet with you to go over the will."

"I thought we were gonna do that tomorrow? Why wasn't he here? Why would he call you?" Rose huffed out of frustration.

"Your cell was off so he called the hotel and they put him through to Jeffery and he gave him my number."

Rose put her head in her hands and sighed several times but she recognized the frustration in Jeff's voice. "Sorry, I'm just a little jumpy."

Rose lost her train of thought as they pulled into the circle drive. A grey Rolls Royce with tinted windows partially hidden behind the house caught her eye. "I've never seen one like that before." She pointed to the car.

"Let's hope it belonged to your grandmother." Jeff whistled.

"Why?"

"Because, that's a 1968 Rolls Royce Phantom VI and it's rare."

"I wonder who else needs to hear the reading of my mother's will. And why it has to be done so damn fast."

"Let's go in and find out." Jeff opened the door and took Rose by the hand. She felt awkward with a veil and hat but the sun fought back the night with a steady stream of glowing warmth that threatened to burn as it hovered just above the horizon.

The butler stood ready with the front door wide open. Sonny bolted down the front steps towards Rose. A handkerchief dangled from his fingers as he threw his arms around Rose's neck with no regard for her veil. He sniffed his sympathies then blew into the hankie. Rose placed a firm index finger at his shoulder and pushed him several steps away. It was aggressively dismissive but she didn't care. She had developed a renewed fervor for protecting her family's estate and her mother's good works.

She turned, looked him squarely in the eyes. "We are here, now, can we get on with it?"

Rose, determined not to waste any more valuable time, turned her back to him and followed the butler as he escorted her into the house. Jeff followed obediently.

The library reeked of old age and damp leather. A long table had been set for five, complete with paper and pens. A crystal canister glistened with an amber liquid. Slices of orange and mint floated between the jagged edged ice cubes. The butler's offer of iced tea was accepted. Which in turn made him smile. He then went about his work of closing all the shudders in the room.

Rose walked to the head of the table and pointed as she removed the gloves. And pulled back the veil and peeled off the hat. "Why do you think it's set for five?" She took a long drink of the tea.

"I don't know, a stenographer, maybe." After, naming each of them, "I can't figure who the others would be."

"I don't have any living relatives that I know of."

A door opened and in stepped an older woman with a steno machine. She went about the business of setting up, foregoing even the most mundane of pleasantries. Sonny entered and took his seat. He motioned for Rose to sit next to him.

"Who's the other seat for?" Rose waited for an answer not quite ready to sit.

"It's for Dwayne's Mother, Ms. Chamblee. Your mother had an extremely charitable heart."

"I've heard." Rose picked up the brief and began to leaf through it.

"No peeking," Sonny shook his forefinger at her.

Rose decided she could use a refill of her iced tea. She reached for the canister and was immediately chided by Sonny who motioned for the already approaching butler.

"I can do this myself." Rose kept a firm grip on the crystal goblet.

The butler tilted his head and held out his hand for the glass. Rose handed over the glass, "Who's Rolls is that parked outside?" She watched as the butler made a ceremony of pouring the tea and placing the doily on the table. He pulled the chair out and waited for Rose to sit. She could not recall a time when she'd been treated so respectfully and commandingly at the same time.

"Thank you, Charles." Rose smiled and nodded.

Charles took his post next to the enormous oak buffet.

Sonny looked put out, "the Rolls belongs to another client whom I am not at liberty to discuss. We will get on with this as soon as——"

Dwayne's mother entered the room in a huff pounding her cane against the hardwood floor with each step and dragging Dwayne at arms-length behind her.

"You just can't find reliable help these days. Damn nurse chose not to show up, again! That's why I'm late. And, Rose, please accept my sympathies for your loss and my apologies for not making it to the funeral. At my age I can barely manage to get around by myself let alone with an afflicted man in tow. I didn't miss nothin' did I?"

"No Ma'am. We would not start without you." Sonny commenced with the introductions, "Charles, take Dwayne to the kitchen for some iced tea and cookies."

Jeff spoke up, "I'll take him, if that's alright with Ms. Chamblee?"

She nodded an affirmative as she motioned with her hand for Dwayne to go.

Dwayne lit up like a Christmas tree and clapped his hands repeatedly. He smiled when his eyes met Rose's. She winked, to his delight. Once Dwayne was safely out the door and out of ear shot Sonny cleared his throat and began reading the will.

Half way through the "here-to-fors", Sonny removed his readers.

"Oh, let's just get to the meat of the will." He focused his attention on Rose. "You'll find all's in order. Copies of deeds to properties, listed items such as furniture, jewelry, stock certificates, locations of safety deposit boxes and keys, etc., etc., etc." Sonny waved his hand in the air for emphasis. "Your grandmother left everything to your mother when she passed except the house on Gordon Place, it's a family home that goes back nearly a century. That she left to you independently, for obvious reasons, with the untimeliness of her death she hadn't changed her will from the original one we did for her after you were born. But Elizabeth and Charles left everything they had to you."

"Ms. Chamblee, there is a special gift for Dwayne." Sonny retrieved a velvet box from his brief case. He opened the box to show off a brilliant collection of coins.

"Thems coins?" Ms. Chamblee squinted. "What the devil am I gonna do with a bunch a coins?"

"That bunch of coins, as you put it, in today's market, are valued at over one hundred thousand dollars." Sonny closed the case and slid it toward Dwaynes' mother.

She grabbed the box and pulled it close to her chest. "Dwayne's gonna love 'em. But, I ain't got a clue how to go about selling coins." Ms. Chamblee pulled the coins closer to her chest and gave the velvet a rub.

Rose raised a finger just as Sonny opened his mouth. "Ms. Chamblee, I'm quite sure Sonny would be glad to be of service. Right?"

Sonny cleared his throat and continued. "Rose, if you'll turn to the last page of your documents. There's a transfer of title to a property. You need to sign that and leave it with me. The rest is for you to take."

Rose examined the document. "There's just a legal description. What property is it?"

"Not one you'd be interested in."

"I'll be the judge of that."

Sonny paused, rolled his eyes as if looking for the answer somewhere in his eye sockets. "It's this house."

Rose's mouth dropped as she glared at her attorney. "How is it that I own this house? And what makes you think I will just sign it over to you?"

"It's very simple. My great-grandfather was originally entrusted with the affairs of the estate. He made several independently wise investments. One rather lucrative investment allowed him to purchase this house. When it needed to be updated your grandmother held a note for the expense of that renovation. My family has lived here for generations. When my father died, two years ago, he left it up to me to get the deed cleared. I just need your signature. It's the least you can do for the years of service my family has given to yours."

Rose glared. "How dare you. What your father did, if I'm not mistaken, is against the law. Investing independently, funds that weren't his. Besides, it says right here, in expenses that you've been paid a handsome salary from the profits of my family's estate. After I've had a chance to analyze the entire portfolio, I'll tell you what needs to be done. What other property do I own?"

Sonny, now red in the face, fumbled through several pages of the will.

"There's the lake house at Altoona. It's a run-down mess. The house you grew up in on Gordon Place and then, there's the house in Savannah. A cottage. It's in good enough shape. We keep it rented during the summer months. It pays for itself."

"I want keys to all my properties by tomorrow evening, including this one. Then I'll let you know how I plan to proceed." Rose gathered her things and left the room.

In the foyer Dwayne squealed, "Rose. Look. Cookies." He held out a palm coated with crumbs and chocolate.

"That's great Dwayne." Rose smiled at Jeff as he handed Dwayne a napkin. "You'll want to go inside." She touched Dwayne's chubby cheek with her fingers. "Your mother has something very special for you. I think you'll like it."

"You gonna go away? You my bestest friend." Dwayne hung his head.

"No. I have too much to do here." She stepped closer to Dwayne and raised her hand to move a lock of hair hanging over his left eye. He closed his eyes tight then grinned.

Dwayne half danced toward the library with the butler close behind.

Rose thought about Dwayne. Even though she couldn't remember a single moment, she could see that for him nothing had changed. He would forever be that little boy and in his eyes she would always be that little girl. She had to wonder what the Rose was like that was locked away in his childlike mind and what other things he may know.

Once outside, Rose looked around for the Rolls. It was gone.

"What's wrong?" Jeff put his hand on Rose's shoulder.

"I can't put my finger on it; it's just a funny feeling in my gut."

"Ms. Bodin!" A voice echoed from across the street.

Rose turned to see a photographer creeping out of the bushes, flanked by at least half a dozen more. Two cars idled on either side of the only exit.

She shouted back, her hands cupped around her mouth, "No comment!"

Jeff yelled over the roar of the engine, "get in."

Rose yanked open the drivers' side door, "scoot over, I'm driving." She backed up the car so it faced out the driveway toward the wave of reporters and photographers. She revved the engine to let them know she meant business. She hit the gas, released the brakes in a sudden motion. The tires spun wild on the red brick and the car slid a few feet left then right before traction catapulted it forward. The reporters dove into bushes and even trashcans to avoid becoming road kill. Rose laughed as she laid black marks on the street in front of the house. Two photographers snapped away at the back of the car. One guy jumped into a white sedan and gave chase.

Adrenaline rushed through rose's veins. Her head pulsed with the excitement and her heart beat hard against her ribcage. She took several deep breaths then looked at Jeff who had a white knuckled grip on the door handle.

"You know, I've always wanted to be a race car driver," Rose laughed.

Jeff grunted, "you are a race car driver."

Several miles of break neck speed and Rose elected to slow the car. She glanced at the traffic behind her through the rearview mirror.

"I think I lost 'em."

Something caught Jeff's attention in the side mirror. The white sedan barreled towards them from a side street.

"Look out!" Jeff grabbed the dash.

Rose jerked the steering wheel to the left into oncoming traffic then back to the right narrowly missing a UPS truck. The driver raised his middle finger in salute. The sedan renewed its' chase.

"I think I can lose this clown somewhere by the freeway."

Jeff tugged on his seat belt to make sure it was secure. The sun had begun to set and streetlights began to flicker in anticipation of the coming dusk.

The cars swerved in and out of traffic for several miles. The business district gave way to dilapidated houses and abandoned shops. Dark and empty pot-holes, evidence of years of neglect, were overshadowed by the dark desperate eyes that peered out from behind broken windows and paint peeled doors. Snotty nosed kids who ran across dirt yards without shoes. And the occasional old man sitting in a metal chair on his porch watching his last days pass by.

"Eureka an escape route!" Rose made a hard left down an alley between a theatre and an abandoned grocery store.

From the opposite end of the street the sedan appeared. Rose hit the brakes hard bringing the car to a screeching halt. The car flashed its' headlights in response.

Jeff huffed. "He wants to play chicken?"

"I doubt it. What he wants is a photo of me doing something crazy."

"Driving like a maniac, perhaps."

"Yeah, but he hasn't gotten a clear shot of me and I don't plan on giving him one." Rose's body shook with an icy chill, tiny beads of sweat appeared on her upper lip, she was more than accustomed to this chill. It meant one thing, trouble.

From a bush-obscured driveway, the grey Rolls Royce glided into the middle of the street between the white sedan and the Lexus. The blacked-out tint on the windows gave the car an ominous appearance.

Rose shook her head in disbelief. "Jeff, that's the car we saw at Sonny's."

"One of a kind, for sure."

"No mistaken' it."

The Rolls blocked the sedan from advancing.

Rose put her car into gear and inched forward to gauge a response.

The white sedan became impatient and revved his engine. It began to inch closer to the other car and showed no signs of surrender. The sedan squealed its' tires and gunned for the silent grey intruder. Seconds before impact the sedan slammed on its' brakes, spun to the left, narrowly missing it. A red-faced reporter with bulging veins shouted obscenities out the open driver's window as he executed a U-turn next to the Rolls. The Rolls remained dead calm.

Rose eased her car into reverse. After backing away several feet, and with no reaction from the remaining car, she turned the wheel and eased the car gently away from the street.

Then she slammed the car into drive and plunged her foot onto the accelerator. Rose peered into the side view mirror just as the driver of the Rolls opened his door. All she saw was a leg in black slacks but it made her stomach dip like the first drop of a roller coaster ride.

The Lexus squealed to a stop just before it entered the crosswalk. Rose's hands hurt from gripping the steering wheel. "I think the freeway is just ahead." Rose adjusted herself, tugged at her seat belt, "Did you get a look at who got out of that car?"

"No. But I'd say it's a stroke of luck that someone intervened."

"Oh, come on. Look around. Who lives in a neighborhood like this and drives a vintage 1968 Rolls Royce with black out tint that just happened to be parked at Sonny's office moments before the chase started? How could he know where we'd end up? It's too much to be a coincidence." Her body shook at the thought. No one could've known where she'd be or where the chase would lead.

How could he've been at the right place at the right time?

"You keep saying 'he', like you know who's driving? Do you?"

"No."

"I think this vampire stalker thing has gotten to that active imagination of yours." Jeff reached over and placed his hand on Rose's hand. She relaxed and smiled.

"Let's go back to the hotel."

Jeff sat back in the seat and stretched out his legs. "Nice driving."

Rose turned the car onto the entrance ramp of the freeway and headed toward town. After several moments of silence, she looked at Jeff, "I can't explain how I got us so close to the house before. It felt like something was tugging at my gut."

"Hm. A memory?"

"It's not a memory, exactly. The only word I can use to describe it is urgency, like I had to get there or suffer a consequence. Or maybe I'm just losing my mind."

"Consequence?" He turned to Rose his eyebrows formed into one long line of concern.

"Yeah. I know. It sounds crazy. Want to know what else is crazy?"

"Always."

"I own Sonny's house."

"How is that possible?"

"His father took some liberties with my family's money and bought the place, but had to borrow from my family to pay for renovations."

Jeff thought for a moment, "Isn't that illegal?"

"I'm sure it is. He claimed it was for investment purposes but now he wants me to sign the deed over to him. I demanded keys to that house and the other ones. They could already be at the hotel."

"How many houses?"

"As of right now three. One is a cabin in Savannah."

Tired from the ordeal, Rose couldn't bring herself to talk anymore about what had happened at the reading of the will.

It's better to wait till I have a handle on things.

For fear of running into more reporters Rose steered the car into the delivery garage at the hotel then handed the keys to the security guard. He directed them to the service elevator.

Once at the door of her suite Rose invited Jeff to come in with one stipulation, he had to mix the drinks.

Rose closed her bedroom door and began to peel the black clothes of mourning off her still trembling body. She could hear ice tinkling into glasses and felt an ease wash over her at the thought of Jeff being, even a little, domestic. Someone knocked softly at the front door. She could hear muffled voices.

She didn't have the strength to shower so she donned a robe and slippers. She eased her aching body onto the sofa next to Jeff then took a long swig of her drink.

"Nobody does it like you." She giggled. The tired, deeper than usual sexy resonation in her voice made her feel uncomfortable.

A quick change of conversation should do the trick.

"Who was at the door?"

"Bellman, he delivered the keys." Pointing to the table where a bundle of keys tied with a red ribbon sat.

Rose took another long drink of her whiskey with a splash of ginger ale and leaned back into the sofa cushion, "maybe I should hold a press conference or something."

Jeff shook his head, "No need. I'll send out a statement. Besides, you've got a press junket starting in a few weeks for the release of Midnight."

"I need time to sort through this." An idea blossomed that made her sit straight up, "I have a cabin in Savannah!"

"Yeah?"

Rose's eyes danced. "That's not a bad thing?"

"I can see the plot thickens." Jeff raised an eyebrow and did a tah-dah with his hands.

Rose leaned forward her drink cupped in her hands. "Wanna go to Savannah?"

Chapter Fifteen

J eff abruptly pulled off the road and came to a halt. He looked deep into rose's blue/grey eyes. She looked away. He stroked her hair, then her face. His thumb under her chin, he lifted her face to within inches of his.

Every inch of her body rose to meet him, anticipation morphed into desire. *Kiss me, please.* Rose closed her eyes expecting him to plant one on her lips. He smiled, "We're here."

"Thank heavens! I thought we'd never get here." Rose played off the disappointment.

"It wasn't that far, only 3 and half hours. I-75 to 16 to Tybee Island, now from Dallas it could be a bit of a trek. I guess that's why we're here, to find out if it's worth it."

Jeff drove the car down the narrow, gravel driveway to the beachfront bungalow. A postcard scene beckoned for them to come. The moss-hung trees in the front hid the house from view of passing cars. The house had seen its years of usage but the view of the water was all together ancient.

The inside of the cabin sparkled in a stark contrast to the plain, A-frame shape outside. With overstuffed sofas, antique quilts and natural wood everything, it was ready for a cover shot in Better Homes and Gardens magazine. The room smelled of fresh flowers and loving attention, not the dank and dusty smell of abandonment that Rose had expected. Jeff opened several windows and a cross breeze brought in the saltiness of the not too-distant ocean. The rock fireplace centered on the back wall was already brimming with firewood.

"This place is in pristine condition. Do you think someone knew we were coming?"

"Did you make sure someone hadn't leased the place?"

"Sonny said it was always ready. I gave him a call just to make sure." Rose engaged her cell, "Damn, no signal. I'll go outside to see if I can get more bars."

She held the phone in the air above her head and walked in circles, made her way to the far side of the cabin but the trees were even thicker. She walked keeping her eyes on the bars of the cell phone, until she stumbled over something hitting the ground so hard the phone flew from her grasp.

A male voice barked, "Hey watch where you're goin' lady!"

Rose jumped to her feet quickly so not to appear weakened by the fall.

"Who are you?" Rose looked around for the catapulted cell phone.

"I'm Jimmy, the caretaker of this here property and I'd say you'd be a trespasser."

"No, I'd say I'm the owner of this property."

"You don't . . . what's your name?"

"Rose Bodin."

"Well, I guess you'd be right to be here." The man wiped his hands on his coveralls then extended one as a peace offering and an introduction.

Rose did the same, "It's a pleasure to meet you, Jimmy."

He nodded in the direction of the phone lying near a shovel, "You ain't gonna get no signal out here. Some places in town are okay but not this far out, too many trees. So, are you here checking things out or what? Mr. James didn't tell me anyone's a comin'. I hope ever' things to your liking."

"The place looks amazing."

"I keep the grounds. It's my wife, Charlene that cleans the inside. She fusses too much but guests seem to like the way she does things."

"You're not expecting anyone else?"

"No Ma'am. Not till later in the year closer to summer. Charlene just likes to do a spring cleaning so I'd say you timed your visit just right."

"Rose, where are you?" Jeff called as he stepped around the cabin into sight.

Rose made the necessary introductions. The two men began a conversation about the level of fishing one could expect. Rose bent down to retrieve her phone. An icy breeze swept up from the ground and slapped her face. She recoiled from it, stumbled backwards, Jeff grabbed her arm steadying her.

"Evidently, I'm more accustomed to flat ground and concrete." Rose shook her head.

"Obviously," Jeff chuckled.

"I think I should go inside now before I do any real damage to myself. Besides, it's getting cold and I could use a fire in that gorgeous fireplace."

They said goodnight to the caretaker and headed for the cabin.

Rose could smell dinner as she exited the bedroom where she had showered and changed into her sweat pants and t-shirt. The aromas awakened her appetite. She quickly towel-dried her hair, a tad, then made her way into the kitchen. On the bar sat an opened bottle of red wine with one filled glass. At the sink Jeff was pouring something into a strainer while two other pots bubbled on the stove.

"Well, hello there. I poured you some wine. I think you'll like it. There is a good stock of wines in the back of the pantry." He picked up his own half empty glass and tilted it toward her, "Here's to your health." And he took a big gulp.

Rose sipped the wine. He was right she did like it.

"So, what are you concocting over there?"

"My bachelor-hood staple, lemon pepper shrimp and pasta with green beans and garlic toast. The pantry is stocked and so is the fridge, but besides a tuna surprise and fried eggs, this is all I can cook."

"It smells great."

"Thanks, I hope it tastes as good."

It did. They ate several helpings each and started on the second bottle of wine for dessert.

The roaring fire let off an amber glow with a phantasm of flickering shadows. They worked together, without saying a word, to clean the dishes. Jeff purposed a high-five and Rose delightfully accepted. As their hands touched, they failed to separate. Rose's hands small and slender against his long fingers and broad palm paled. His fingers tenderly folded around hers and he pulled her into his chest. He kissed her forehead in a delicate way that made a fire erupt inside of Rose. She looked up to look into his eyes and there she saw a reflection of her own desire.

"Well, it would seem we have more than just a business relationship at hand." She giggled nervously. Her eyes refused to move from his. She ached.

"I didn't think you had any romantic feelings towards me. And, if it's just the emotion of the trip and what you've been through, I can back off. I don't want to confuse you or mislead you."

"How could you mislead me?"

"You need to know that no matter what this turns out to be I will always be here for you. I don't do one-night stands, so if that's all you need, I will step aside."

"No. I have always loved you. You're my best friend. We've been through so much the last 15 years. I've been so self-absorbed with my issues and all this that I forgot to consider my heart. You have always been there. It's always been you."

He kissed her passionately then held her so close Rose could feel all the broken pieces inside her come together. Her cheek nestled against his chest felt so right she could've stood in the kitchen forever.

"I need to sit down. The wine is taking hold."

Jeff released her and followed her to the sofa. They sat close talking and kissing and touching until Rose yawned and laid her head on his lap.

A sound jolted her. She sat up. Looking around the room she couldn't place what the sound was. Her heart slowly began to return to its' normal rhythm. Nothing appeared out of place. The fire had died down but the flickering ash let off a faint orange glow. Then she heard a moan. As she leaned over she heard the moan again. It was Jeff, asleep on the sofa next to her. His legs curled up tight. Rose lighted from the sofa and crouched on her knees to the floor. She crawled to where Jeff's head rested seemingly peacefully, albeit noisily.

His eyes flickered. His head turned from one side to the other. He moaned. Rose curled up her knees and leaned her back against the sofa. She watched as Jeff fought with whatever demon there was in his dream. She longed to touch his face, to feel the warmth of him against her. So close, she could smell him. His cologne mingled with the wine, he smelled like a man, not the imaginary ones she wrote about. She closed her eyes to revel in his scent a little longer. He moved another moan escaped. This time he looked to be in distress. His eyebrows crushed tight and his lips pressed inward. He tossed his head back and forth. Rose got up on her knees and leaned over him. She placed a hand on his chest in an attempt to quiet him. He stiffened and then sat straight up. Both his hands were on her as fear danced in his eyes. He shouted, "Rose!" The realization of who was touching him crossed his face. His lips parted and he sighed.

He wrapped his arms around her so tight she could barely catch a breath. In reaction Rose put her hands on his back and rubbed.

She whispered into his ear, "It's okay, it was just a dream."

He leaned back and cupped her face in his hands, "I will never let anything happen to you."

"Really? So, you're my body guard now too?" She chuckled.

He pulled her to him and kissed her gently at first on the corner of her lips then whispered several more across her mouth with the kind of passion that could make her forget her own name. His tongue explored every inch of her mouth and neck leaving no room for doubt about his intentions. He lifted her off the floor and against his warm, hard body. She could feel his already swollen manhood rising beneath her. She relaxed her body, as she melted around every part of him. They kissed. The rough of his whiskers stung but in a pleasurable way that would not allow her to pull away.

Jeff rubbed his hands up and down her hips. He adjusted her so that his erection found a niche between her pelvic bone and thigh. He moaned. Her nipples reacted to the reverberation in his chest. She couldn't halt the urge to slide up and down over him to feel him moan again. He grabbed her, tight, and stopped moving. She looked down into his pleading eyes, "What?"

Jeff swallowed hard, "I can't take much more. I want you."

Rose looked him square in the eyes, "I want you, now."

Jeff sat up cradled Rose in his arms. In one swift, effortless motion they were off the sofa and headed for the bedroom.

Beside the bed Jeff took off his shirt. Rose sat up on her knees the bed making her a perfect height to greet the tender space between his Adam's apple and chest. They kissed indulgently as hands roamed. Jeff pulled at the t-shirt. Rose felt a chill across her breasts hardening her nipples. He pressed his body to hers engulfing her completely. His tongue kept up a passionate rhythm with hers. One hand explored her full breast the other grabbed her buttocks. He released her lips and with one hand on her back he used his weight to lay her down onto the quilted comforter of the queen size bed. Her legs instinctively wrapped around his waist, she instinctively squeezed. He licked her nipples, then used his breath to dry them only to moisten them over and over. Rose whimpered with anticipation. She pressed her hands against his lower back just above his butt cheeks trying to force him inside her. She wanted him more than she'd ever wanted anyone. Then he kissed her ribs, her belly, his tongue danced in circles on her inner thigh. It was too much for her to bear, she whispered, "Please."

Jeff placed himself deep inside her quivering warmth. Neither one moved for a moment, waiting for the world to come to a sudden and abrupt end. Rose tilted her pelvis upward. Jeff pumped and groaned. Rose reached for his rhythm and found it, together, in-sync as they had always been.

Jeff shook and quivered until every inch of his body had consumed hers. They lay next to each other, depleted of energy, and without words.

Rose wanted to tell him she'd never felt this before and she wanted to feel it again and again. Tears trickled down to sweaty hair. His kisses were softer and sweeter. With flushed cheeks and weighted eye-lids she wanted sleep. Her head in the crook of his arm, her body warm against his, she went limp. Her rambling thoughts were that they had a lifetime to make love and that thought lulled her into a deep sleep.

Chapter Sixteen

ose opened her eyes to blackness. Thick headed and cloudy, her body stirred slightly, lazily. The right hand resisted the brains request for movement so she commanded only the forefinger. It jerked but what she felt under her finger was not fabric, she did not lay in a warm bed, this was cold, grainy. *It's dirt!*

The realization shot through her body electrifying each cell into defense mode. Hands in front of her eyes she could now feel satin fabric only inches from her face. Her bare heels dug several inches into dirt. With all her might she heaved at the covering. A tiny bit of light, red and diffused, shot in for a second but she now knew she was in a coffin. With a screaming effort Rose flung the lid open. It resonated with an eerie hollowness as it strained against the hinges. Rose sucked in hard, gasped as much air as her lungs would hold. She looked around, alone, hand on her chest to make sure there was still a heartbeat. She looked down no longer wearing the light blue polo shirt of Jeff's . . .

Oh God, where is Jeff?

Rose's mind searched in desperation for a memory or a thought that would tell her why she was lying in dirt...*a dirt filled coffin!*

She hurled her leg first and then the rest of her body came out and onto the cobble stone floor. Shadows flickered. Light from a dozen or more candles burned in scattered groups around the room. Completely purged of sleepiness

Rose took stock of her surroundings. First, the dark redwood coffin was not fancy but had a rather ornate emblem on the top. Rose closed the lid to get a better look at it. In the center a lion on two legs wore a crown and a cape. Under the lion two swords crossed and above the lion a crested moon with a star. She could not even imagine what it meant. A family crest, maybe, but something told her it was much more ominous. She lifted the lid again and examined the dirt she'd been lying on. Instinct forced her to put her hand on top of the pile. It was soft and warm. Not black dirt, brown but with a red tint to it, perhaps a little clay mixed in. In one corner of the room a round wooden table with lions' heads carved on the legs stood regally dressed with a fur runner puddled to the floor. On that were several bowls and very pretty chalices decorated with colorful jewels. In bowls, all kinds of fruit that made her mouth water. Rose backed away from the coffin and looked around. The walls donned heavy, woven tapestries.

Several depicted hunting scenes, men on horseback, rabid looking hounds with snarled snouts. There was a familiarity to it, like the one on the wall of the book signing but different. Another one, on the farthest wall and much smaller than the others, was of the Virgin Mary holding the Christ Child and still another, behind a curved portion of wall, was the Crucifixion of Christ. The floor of cobblestone had a worn look to it as if it were very old the stones worn to a smooth luster. There were no windows or doors that she could see so she walked around the room hitting the walls trying to find a way out. She discovered an old pot in one far off corner and assumed that was her pot to piss in. She shivered at the thought.

After searching for a way out with no luck Rose went back to the table and the fruit. She extended a hand to one of the cups, it was heavy her hand trembled. Her left hand grabbed the right then she began to tremble all over. She sniffed expecting to smell red wine but there was no smell. Could it be water? It appeared dark but maybe it was the cup that was dark and it made the water appear red. She tapped the cup it rippled like water she sipped it. The liquid was cold, wet and sweet. Whatever it was it was what she needed. Instantly the fruit in the bowl shriveled turned dark and unappealing. Rose stepped away from the table. In the distance, a very large dog howled. Her spine tingled and she turned her body in the direction of the sound. The howling grew stronger and closer. The next howl sounded like it was outside her room. She replaced the cup to the table and walked in the direction of the howling. With both hands she began to pound on one of the tapestries lining the walls until she discovered a hollow sound that echoed. Rose grabbed the heavy fabric and ripped it from its' rusting iron rod. Behind it, an arched wooden door with reinforced black metal hinges. Rose laughed until she brought tears to her eyes.

"What the hell is this, a Bela Lugosi movie set? You've got to be fucking kidding me!" She yelled for help but no one answered. She banged on the door for what felt like hours. Her knuckles ached and the skin began to crack and bleed. After a few whacks at it with the palms of her hands she resigned to just sit. Someone would come? Maybe whoever left the fruit would come back?

It has to be the stalker from the hotel, the one who thinks he's my vampire Constantine. I don't know how he did that levitation thing but he's gone overboard this time.

A shadow slithered across the cobblestones. The candles flickered wildly. Rose closed her eyes tight and pulled her knees into her chest. She began to whimper as she felt a cold breeze.

The shadow became a figure. It was Constantine. Without a disturbance of air, he was suddenly within inches of her face. His slender frame was well proportioned his overall appearance striking. Black wavy hair and deep-set eyes should have made him a hunk but the paleness of his skin and yellow in his eyes gave him up as a monster. He reached out his hand to her. Shaking, she placed her fingertips in his palm. He effortlessly lifted her to her feet.

"I see you drank a portion of the blood I left for you."

"That was blood? Liar!" Rose gagged at the very thought.

"Oh, so melodramatic my little changeling. Blood tastes different to you and I. It is sweet and satisfying. Like a tall cold glass of water use to taste when we were human." He stroked her cheek with an icy finger. She jerked back.

"I am human."

"You do not still believe that?"

"I believe that you're a freak and you've kidnapped me. You'll never get a ransom. The Feds will find you and blow your freaky ass to smithereens." Rose trembled but tried to sound sure and confident. She felt weak and small.

He laughed a thundering roar. "I am Constantine. I will never age or die from sickness. I am vampire."

"You are not! I made you up. Constantine is just a character in my books. Vampires don't exist you psychotic creep."

Constantine picked up the challis and turned it over the liquid splattered on the stone thick and crimson. It was blood!

Rose stumbled back against the coffin purged what little she had swallowed. With blood dripping from her chin she screamed, "What do you want?"

"I am going to feed you. Soon you will be purged of all your humanness. You and I will rule the night together, for eternity."

"I am human! Blood will only make me wretch and you can't make me drink it!"

"I will not have to make you. You will get thirsty and you will get hungry and you will beg for me to feed you."

"Never, you prick!"

"Never? There is no such thing." He blew her a kiss and was out the door before Rose could take one step.

Chapter Seventeen

Rose woke to the tinkling of ice in a glass. Her eyes burned as she strained to see the source. Skin tugged and her lips tore at the corners when she opened her mouth. The dryness in her throat prevented her from taking a deep breath. Her head ached and knees knocked forcing her to grab the table leg for support.

"Oh, Cheri, you do look haggard. Please drink. After just a sip you yanked that tapestry off the iron rod as if it were mere linen. Imagine what you could do if you nourished your body with the one thing it craves."

She struggled to get up and fell back to the floor.

"I will make you stronger."

"Water, please." The words clawed their way out of her mouth.

"Only blood. I should have changed you when I had the opportunity."

Rose watched as he left the room. *Did he shut the door?* Unsure, she dragged her body to the door. *It's open!*

Rose grabbed the door latch and pulled herself up. Without some source of sustenance she would not be able to escape. The days had blended together; with no sunlight she couldn't be sure how long she'd gone without food or water. She turned back toward the table. A fresh goblet and a new bowl of fruit rested on the table. *I have no choice. Eat or die.*

She staggered back to the table and grabbed at the fruit. Grapes, nectarines, plums and bananas burst in her mouth. The juice ran down her chin and fingers dripped with pulp. She ate wildly and indiscriminately, chewing on rind and pith as well as seeds. Her mouth could not close completely but she swallowed as much and as fast as she could. Before giving a second thought Rose grabbed the goblet and drank. The liquid burned going down her parched throat like a young Merlot before it's had time to breath.

"Noooo!" She threw the cup away from her, watched in horror as blood splattered. The fruit made an early departure from her stomach tinted with the blood.

God I've got to get out of here.

Her skin turned supple. She raised her hand in time to see her fingernails grow thick and strong. Hair flowed and lips moistened. Both breasts began to tingle with life. The feeling of energy overwhelmed her. She turned to the door.

Run!

Running through the narrow passages Rose could hear the breeze whistle in her ears. She had never run this fast. She had never had to run for her life. She tried door handles as she flew passed them but all were locked. A staircase, she dashed down the stone steps barely touching each one. A door ajar. She burst through looking for an escape or at the least fresh air. Just a few feet in front of her, dangling from a chain attached to the ceiling, hung Jeff. Rose let out a scream, a mournful wail, as she went to her knees.

He hung upside down, below his head a jeweled challis. Blood dripped slowly from a small wound on his neck. His skin pale, eyes closed, he hung so still he appeared to be dead. Rose reached out her hand, he moaned.

"Jeff, it's me, Rose. Can you hear me? Are you alive? I need to get you down from here. Hold on, I'll get you down." She crawled to him and lifted his head.

He was so heavy. She stood and stepped behind him then ran her fingers along the chain that traveled from his wrist to his ankles and then on up to a hook in the ceiling. There was no way for her to release him.

Applause resonated from behind her. Rose jerked. From behind a hanging gilded cage Constantine stepped clapping in approval.

"Brava darling."

"Get him down! You maniac, what have you done to him?"

"I had to feed you. You had to have good strong human blood. I really thought by now you would have had more of his blood and been able to appreciate my macabre sense of humor and be strong enough to lift his dying body from the hook. Alas, you are still too weak." He reached to touch her. She slapped his hand away.

"Umm," Jeff opened his eyes to a slit. He pleaded for her to go with what little expression he could afford.

"No." Rose sobbed, "I can't just leave you like this. Don't ask me to. Jeff, I'm sorry." She touched his cheek, his head rolled toward her hand, his flesh felt cold.

Constantine chuckled. Rose looked up and screamed, "you bastard," as she charged. He deflected her punch knocking her to the cold floor with a twitch of his wrist.

"You could be as strong as me if you would only allow me to dispose of your humanness. Give in to the inevitable. It does not hurt, much. It is as easy as going to sleep and you wake a new creature. You will submit soon enough or I can take you now." He growled and lunged for her.

Rose twisted to her feet and ran from the room and up another 3 sets of stairs. She found an open door leading to a sitting room. Inside she could see that every inch of the wall space was covered with art, musical instruments and books. A red velvet sofa invited her to sit but she collapsed in a sobbing heap her face buried in a satin pillow.

Chapter Eighteen

onstantine entered and sat in a chair by her head his legs crossed poised for a fireside chat.

"Rose, I know how hard this is for you because of your high spiritedness but I assure you, not only am I real but the legend of vampire is very real. You did not make me up as you so eloquently phrased it. I gave you stories about me to write so that you would understand and be sympathetic when your time came to change fully. So, while you rest, I will give you the answers to some of your questions about your childhood. First, you must understand how it all began. Hunters, slayers, if you will, pursued me. In those days I was young and arrogant. Not feeding for several days had weakened me. They attacked at the first light of dawn burning my illustrious mansion to the ground. I barely escaped. I lunged and clawed my way through the brush until I found that abandoned fence post along your property line. I clung to it and gasped for air.

The sun burned. Darkness would not come for hours. I could not have escaped the hunters. Their familiarity with the woods gave them the advantage. If only I had fed, the aroma of their fear would have awakened me long before those imbeciles could have gained access to my private burial chamber. I watched as my sanctuary for the last 300 years lit the purple pink sky with plumes of white and gray smoke.

Tiny rays of sunlight burned my dried and browning flesh. I had to find a source of blood and get out of the light. You understand, with my drying eyes and crumbling fingertips I must have looked like a monster. I made my way to the magnolia. I crawled underneath the protective limbs where no sunlight penetrated. The earth, soft and musty, cooled my flesh.

Your sweet, tender voice paralyzed me. Your scent was ambrosia. I was not certain I could control you in my weakened condition but I knew I should not kill you.

A ball burst into my shadowy lair. My cat like reflexes forced the ball back with just a flick of my withering wrist. I felt relieved that I had not lost all my vampiric abilities. The limbs of the tree parted with even less effort. You approached with the confidence of my equal. Evidence you felt no fear. When our eyes met you smiled, and excitedly spoke one word, 'Hey'.

You were stunning with your big blue/grey eyes. Your checks flush with life. I could smell the blood feast within you. I waved my fingers in front of your eyes and watched as they glazed over, such is the way of all my victims. I believe now that I actually felt a twinge of remorse. But that is only in retrospect you see.

All I needed was a small drink of your precious blood to give me the strength to escape. I knew to be careful. Your jugular pulsed with invitation. Your delicate skin gave way as if it yielded to me out of pity. Your blood flowed into my mouth in pulsating currents. My vision began to clear, my skin became pliable and my hair smoothed back into a fine mane of ebony. A moan from deep inside you warned me. I feared I had gone too far, taken too much. I bit my own lip and pressed my bleeding flesh against your mouth. Just a couple of drops, that is all you would need. You gagged at first but within a few seconds you swallowed. You licked your lips. Content I had neither killed you nor changed you I left you there to slumber in the protective cover of the sweet Magnolia tree. I looked back at your angelic face and yearned for more. I vowed to return later, after I had dispatched the hunters.

So, you see my darling it is useless for you to deny your true self. You are of my blood, my kin so to speak. I could have killed you, taken you with me, raised you as my forever daughter but I wanted a companion not an underling. Changing one so young could have resulted in dire consequences. It is not so easy for a young mind and heart to deal with eternity. They can go mad and then feed into a deadly frenzy whereby they can lose their mind and walk into the sunlight or get captured and murdered. I felt curiosity at how I could mold you and yet allow you time to mature. I came up with a brilliant plan. I worked hard and planned for this time in our lives. We can be together forever if you accept the gift. You must drink and continue to purge yourself of what remains of your humanity. Your strength was impressive tonight. I always knew you would make a fine partner. Rest for now. I will return before dawn to make sure you are comfortable." Constantine left the way he always had with little fanfare and no noise. Rose dug her face into the pillow.

If that is what happened and he is a vampire, why can't I remember any of it?

Exhausted Rose drifted off to sleep.

Nightmares plagued her sleep. In her dream Rose ran, not knowing where to or what from. She just ran. Fingers poked and grabbed at her. She ran faster until, finally, darkness. She felt her body spiral down deeper into the nightmarish sleep that ensnared her.

She screamed, arms flailed and fingers groped looking for something to stop her from falling when her body hit hard, catapulting her out of her dream state.

Gasping for air she lifted her cheek from the carpeted floor. Eyes blurred but a figure began to take shape several feet from her. Her right hand lifted.

"Help me," squeaked out of her dry throat.

The voice replied with such compassion, "I am here. Come to me." A hand, palm up, appeared before her.

Without trepidation she reached out. Her body lifted then settled upon a cold, firm lap. Rose curled her legs up to her chest and placed both feet upon his knee. Constantine wrapped both arms around her and pulled her tighter against his chest.

"This was worth the wait of a thousand years."

"How long was I asleep?"

"A few days, a few nights no one is keeping count."

Blood-tinged tears fell to his shirt as she wept.

"That is it my beloved. Allow your humanity to depart. It will not be long now."

Rose cried for what felt like hours. "You bit me? I am becoming a vampire?"

"Yes. Albeit slowly."

Thoughts crept through her jagged mind; the foster kids that teased her and foster parents who feared her, the look of pity on JoAnne's face when she first caught sight of the poor, little orphan who so desperately needed a mother and Jeff's eyes as they pleaded for death. Rose could fight no more. She wanted to lie in the coffin forever like her mother, Elizabeth. Rose missed Elizabeth. She wept harder. So much time lost. So much love and warmth gone now there would be only coldness and hunger. Had her mother suffered? Had she clawed her own throat?

"How could she do such a barbaric thing to herself?" Rose hadn't realized she asked the question out loud.

"She did no such thing to herself. I put an end to her madness. She had out lived her usefulness. Had she embraced her role as a familiar she may have fared better." Constantine sighed expelling a heavy rancid breath.

Rose stopped crying, there were no more tears. The recollection of her mother's warmth, the love she felt that day, grew stronger from deep inside Rose. The memory of her mother's last words resonated, 'You have the power.'

"I have the power?"

"Yes, you have the power. You only need more blood. Then, when you are stronger I can teach you to hunt with —" The slap across his face halted any other attempt at words.

"Monster!" Rose pushed herself out of his lap. Clad only in a white linen nightgown and running faster than even before, she felt more alive than ever. The cold air penetrating the thin fabric pricked her nerves into action. Determined to find a way out, determined to live, she ran up and down every staircase trying every door. *Go up!*

At the top of the sixth set of stairs Constantine posed, he laughed and with a blink he was next to her, her arm in his grip. "You really think you can just scamper away. Come now, my pet, let me show you just how hopeless this endeavor of yours truly is."

He allowed Rose to yank her arm from his grip. She took two steps but Constantine, already two steps ahead of her, laughed. He walked in a fluid and precise way. They came to a glass door covered with steam.

"A sauna? Really? You don't approve?"

Rose stared defiantly into his black eyes.

"Your sarcasm is dutifully noted. Now, go in and clean yourself. All that human business is messy and you still reek of it. I shall have a surprise for you when you have completed your bath." He leaned in and kissed her forehead. So slight, the kiss, Rose barely felt it but for the chill it left on her skin.

Rose heaved the heavy glass door. It glided open and then slowly shut behind her. Through the steam she could see glistening water from a roman-style bath. On a bamboo chair were necessary items, soap, a washcloth, a towel and a kimono. The linen nightgown, soaked from the steam, now clung to her skin making her feel uncomfortable, naked. She pulled the garment up and over her head. Her body was tighter than before and her breasts as firm as when she was 16. With her hands cupping her breasts she explored their roundness. She could feel herself responding to the touch.

Rose closed her eyes and sighed, still human. When she opened her eyes, JoAnne stood just inches before her. Rose screamed then covered her breasts with her hands. "How di—"

JoAnne lifted a finger to Rose's mouth then chuckled, "Kitten, I've seen your breasts before, no need to become shy now. Let's get you cleaned up and feeling better." JoAnne led Rose, her mouth still agape, by the elbow toward the entrance of the bath. JoAnne obviously wasn't herself. JoAnne would never have pranced around naked, even with her daughter, in a steam bath owned by a vampire.

"Mom, he's a madman. Did he kidnap you too? He killed Jeff and is trying to make me drink blood he thinks he's a vampire. Why are you here? How did he get you? Do you know how to get out of here?"

"In due time sweetie. Let's get you cleaned up."

Rose lowered her body into the hot scented water. JoAnne, one step behind, settled on a built-in marble bench behind Rose and began squeezing a sponge full of water over her shoulders. It warmed every inch of rose's body. Her skin prickled and she took several deep breaths. Her knuckles still swollen from the door were stinging from the soapy water.

The warmth of physical touch, the water flowing over her skin, she missed these. Her mother's hands were as gentle as she remembered. But Rose pondered the way her mother looked, younger. Didn't JoAnne have little wrinkles around her mouth from years of smoking, and an overall toughness to her skin from years of sun worship? It all seemed so surreal but nothing had been the same since . . .

"Just relax. You've had it hard these past few weeks. But it'll get better. You'll see."

"Mom? Are you real?"

"You betcha, Kitten."

"Then it would probably hurt if I did this." Rose, with both hands grabbed JoAnne's wrist, bit with all her might into the flesh. Blood spurted into her mouth. The metallic taste repulsed her. She spit and gagged as she splashed water into her mouth. Rose turned to face JoAnne. The woman before her had not flinched. Instead, JoAnne extended her bloody wrist to Rose, "You can feed. I would be honored to help you turn. We'd be a real family, a true blood relation."

Rose dove into the water, swimming to the opposite end. The woosh of the water as it passed her ears felt right. Rose prayed that when she came up on the other side all would be back to normal and this would've been a nasty nightmare. But she popped her head out of the water to find JoAnne waiting for her.

"When did you turn, or have you always been a vampire?"

"I'm not a vampire, silly. I'm a familiar. It's a —"

"I know what a familiar is, Mother. I write this shit, remember." Rose shook her head.

"I didn't mean to imply you didn't but to explain my presence here with you now, I must explain our arrangement. I will remain human to assist Constantine. He came to me a year after we moved to Texas. Just a few months after your dad and I adopted you."

"You've always been a familiar? How much of his blood have you had?"

"Only a tad here and there to keep the youthful appearance I am accustom to. And to heal." She pushed at her hair and patted under her chin her wrist was already healed. "His blood does wonders."

"Yeah, we should bottle it. You haven't always been so youthful looking. You were starting to show your age." Rose turned and splashed water on her face.

"Constantine stopped giving his blood to me because he was off preparing things for you. He wanted to be sure I would be willing to sacrifice anything for you. And, I would." JoAnne raised her arm her wrist had already healed. She continued, "Although, I loved you dearly, he offered me eternal life if I would help him. The last time you and I spoke he was with me. Your father didn't understand the benefits and he couldn't handle the whole blood thing. I am sorry for that I did love him." She paused and looked to the ceiling as if sending up a little prayer to the husband she had lost.

"You killed Dad?"

"No. Constantine tried to negotiate with him but unfortunately your father shot himself in the head with his own gun. It's all for the better. Your dad could never have gotten accustom to this life."

"So, everything, everyone I've ever known or loved has been a lie?" *Except Jeff.*

"No. Your life has been sheltered and well groomed." With that JoAnne reached out her hand to stroke Roses face, the bite marks on her wrist were now healed. Rose sank away from the touch.

"The only way to escape this is to die?"

"Only the human part of you has to die. If you would just give in and drink, purge yourself of the aging, rotting humanity inside you. I want you to live forever. He made me this way so that I could help. Please, let me help you." JoAnne clasped her hands together pleading.

"If this is my destiny then it won't hurt to tell me where we are?"

"You should know it's your home. Now, let's see about getting your hair washed and conditioned."

Rose swam away from JoAnne then stopped. "Would you please put on a robe or something, it's just a little too weird to have my naked mother washing my hair in a Roman bath."

"Of course." Once she had donned a toga JoAnne retrieved a challis filled with scented shampoo. Rose let her thoughts go quiet but she knew she could never call JoAnne, mother again. Roses one memory of Elizabeth, her true mother, kept coming back to give her hope, a real tactile hope she felt in her heart.

JoAnne wrapped the big kimono around Rose as she alighted from the water.

"You said 'these weeks' earlier. How long have I been down here?"

"Well let's see, time is very different for me now but I guess for you it would be about eight weeks."

"Isn't anyone looking for me or Jeff?"

"No. Constantine took care of all that when he destroyed the cabin. Everyone thinks you died, a nasty gas leak caused an explosion."

"What about my book? What happened to my book?"

"The publishing house has had it on hold. They are trying to decide whether to publish it with the ending you had last on your computer or to hire a ghost writer to finish it."

"A ghost writer, that's fucking ridiculous. No one can just write the ending of a book for you, those money hungry bastards!" Rose stormed off with JoAnne in tow.

Chapter Nineteen

ose now knew she had something to fight for, her book, no one was going to bank off her talent now that Jeff was most likely dead. No, she had to get the hell out as soon as possible.

Constantine stood in the doorway of her bedroom. "I brought your mother here—"

"She's not my mother. She's your bitch let's keep that straight." Rose pointed her finger at Constantine and then at JoAnne.

"I believe you have offended her yet I am pleased to see the bath has restored you."

"Bull shit."

He took several steps toward Rose and turned, "I have a surprise for you."

"What, werewolves?"

Choosing to ignore the comment Constantine continued. "Tonight, is the anniversary of the day we met. I thought it most fitting that we complete your transformation under the Magnolia, where it all began. Do you like the romance of the idea?"

"Do I get a say?"

"No." He opened the dresser, inside were dozens of dresses. "I'll leave this up to you, surprise me." The weight of the air in the room lifted signaling his departure.

"I'll surprise you."

Rose slipped on the third dress when JoAnne made an entrance. Standing in the doorway, a glass of vodka in one hand the other hand rested on her hip, she shook her head.

"I hope you haven't decided on that one?"

"What do you care? Either way I'm dinner."

"Don't be crass I raised you better than that. Besides, red is so last year. Try the dark blue one it'll bring out your eyes. Men love blue for some reason. I bought it just for you." JoAnne swaggered to the bed and gently sat down her legs crossed at the ankles.

"That must be why it was the first I tried on and the first I trashed." Rose turned to the pile on the floor, the blue satin dress on the bottom.

From the back of the dresser Rose found a big box tainted with years of neglect. She pulled at the lavender ribbon till it fell from the lid. Inside the box, from underneath yellow tissue, Rose could see deep rich purple velvet. Her eyes lit up.

"How absolutely gorgeous, I've never seen anything so delicate." Rose held the dress up to her petit frame then pulled the dress over her head and motioned for JoAnne to help her. JoAnne's hands were like ice from cuddling the glass of vodka. Goose bumps ran a trail up Roses spine. A simple sheer silk, A-line skirt that hung from an Empire waist with scalloped capped sleeves. In the front a split to display a gathering of sheer lilac that matched the sleeves. In the middle of the Empire waist, just under her breast, sat a diamond shaped patch of crystals. The back of the dress was bare and scooped just above Roses derriere. Across the back, at the shoulder blades, were three strands of crystals. Rose spun in circles, "I feel like a princess."

"It was made for a princess." Constantine stood in the hallway just outside the room.

"You look more beautiful than I imagined." He bowed then motioned to JoAnne, "leave us now." She complied without an utterance or a glance. Constantine approached at a slow humanly pace. Then just stood waiting, watching.

"If you're waiting for me to do a trick or something, I won't. This is it."

Her voice trembled. To see him like this was more terrifying than before because he appeared more human than she knew him to be. His stature, intimidating enough but when accompanied by his broad shoulders he was overbearing. His nearly translucent complexion and firm chiseled jaw line, proud forehead and pronounced nose all added to his powerful presence like the marble statue of David. Then he blinked with those amazingly long dark eyelashes caressing marbleized hazel eyes. Every feature slight, even his eyebrows not over grown or wild as one would expect from a monster. His ebony hair caressed his forehead with a rogue strand. His lips parted slightly the left side a little crooked by comparison to the right but in a way that could make him appear boyish if he smiled. A tiny cleft of his chin balanced it all perfectly. He was beautiful. An air of royalty illuminated the room. Rose sucked in the breath she had forgotten. He took a step then another and another. She couldn't have moved if she wanted to. Rose stared transfixed by his features.

Constantine took her hand in his, Rose recoiled at the touch.

He's warm, oh God he's just fed.

He bowed deep took her fingertips lightly on his and brushed his lips across her trembling hand then a quick lick from his pointy tongue. He looked up into her eyes as she removed her hand from his. "My apologies, my intention was not to entrance you. Tonight, I am your teacher."

Rose could feel the blush on her cheeks and chided herself for it then shook the feeling from her head. How can this monster make me feel repulsed and wanting at the same time?

Monster, don't forget.

"Come allow me to escort you to dinner. I think it is the only civil way to start our journey this evening."

"A last supper?" Rose gave a humorless laugh. He did not acknowledge the pun. They walked, her hand resting on top of his open hand down several long corridors. The entire way Rose made note after note of where they could be. The halls were cool and everything reeked of mustiness, the air, the walls and the mirrors. Upon entering the dining-room a chime announced the time.

Candles lit the room with a hazy glow. A circular dinner table sat in the center of the room atop a lion skin rug complete with the lions' head and full mane. The heavy chairs elaborately carved and upholstered were pulled out from the table in an inviting manner. The room brimmed with wild game trophies. A mirror hung forward from the fireplace mantel. The table and its' occupants were duplicated in full view. She gasped and pointed at their reflections, "Vampires have no reflection!"

"I project my image to make you more comfortable, but if you prefer . . ."

"I don't need any favors." Rose shook her head. As she turned to make her way to the chair Constantine was already there, ready to seat her. He unfolded a napkin and placed it onto her lap.

He sat, with a flick of his wrist his napkin snapped onto his lap. "I move more slowly so that you are not startled. I want to reassure so that you are completely at ease. I want the night of your rebirth to be memorable for you."

Rose leaned in, "I don't know what you expect, it's all been memorable for me. You plan to turn me so why all the pomp and circumstance? Just get it over with."

"Indulge me." Constantine's eyes glared.

"Fine. What does one talk about over dinner with a vampire who plans to turn them into one of the undead?"

He took a deep breath, "You are the writer be creative. You must have questions. You may ask whatever you like."

"How the hell do I get out of here? You said you bit me when I was a little girl. Did that make me lose my memory? How much blood did you give me? When exactly will I become a vampire and can I stop it? Will I crave blood right away? When do I get fangs?"

He held up his hands in surrender, "One at a time, please. We have all of eternity. Yes, I did bite you. I needed to escape and you fed me. Your blood was nectar and your spirit like no other humans' I have ever known. I gave you only a taste a mere drop or two of my blood, enough to heal you so that no one would know. You are rare. I have lived millennia and not found anyone I wanted to share this special gift with. Fangs come last. The hunger will come in time but you must first be purged of all your own blood."

"Then why not just drain me?"

"I want to do this gradually it is less painful and I believe more gratifying than the way I was turned. Your memory I shrouded to protect you. I am the only one who can restore it to you," he raised a finger to his lips to shush her, "and that I will do in good time. As you grew, I would come to you at night I took you places and showed you things about vampires and the lives we lead so your books would be unique. You need wealth to exist through centuries. I have enjoyed grooming you for this life. Your sleeplessness has been a result of my having kept you up too late for your human body."

"The sun sensitivity, has that been my imagination?"

"No. As my blood floats through you it is sensitive to the sunlight and it burns your skin in order to get you out of the sun. You would not perish, and no it is not genetic. You are an excellent writer."

"I know. How did you become a vampire?"

"You do not care to hear the ghastly details before dinner."

"Dinner? You're not eating, are you?"

"I did plan on a drink or two." He lifted one eyebrow.

"Touché, I would enjoy a cocktail or would that thin my blood too much for your liking?"

"It will be of no consequence to me. Thank you for asking."

The door opened and in walked JoAnne with a snifter of dark amber liquid atop a silver-serving platter. She placed the glass on the table in front of Rose, "One Grand Marnier, really old." She left with her head held high.

Rose wrapped her hands around the snifter and sat back deep into the chair. "Cheers."

From a dark decanter Constantine poured himself a crimson glass of what Rose assumed had to be blood.

"Salute." He raised his glass slightly and then drank.

"Do you plan to kill JoAnne or turn her too?"

Constantine laughed, "You will need your mother…" he stopped, raised one hand as he put down his goblet, "my apologies, JoAnne, you'll need her to do your bidding and to attend to certain daily chores. Vampires do not make willing valets or ladies in waiting but familiars live to serve. Think of her as my gift to you. If you prefer to make your own valet then JoAnne will make a satisfying first meal."

Rose swallowed hard at the thought of devouring JoAnne, as her hand lightly caressed the gems that dangled freely from her dress.

"You like the diamonds?" Constantine motioned.

"They looked like glass to me but yeah, they're beautiful." She let her one hand fall to her lap and then she took a long drink of the liquor.

Rose cleared her throat, "How much will it hurt?"

"I will be as gentle as I can. It will hurt but nothing worth doing is painless. There must be sacrifice so as to achieve greatness."

"So, being undead and drinking blood and hunting humans is greatness?"

"Living eternally, learning to harness and utilize gifts of power and persuasion are necessary. But it is how you utilize your gifts that will determine your greatness. As for hunting humans, humans hunt deer for sustenance so there is little difference. I do not kill out of revenge or hate or prejudice, only for food or in self-defense."

"You were human once, and now you're the top of the food chain what the hell do you have to defend yourself against?"

"Slayers, jealous vampires, we are not that different and we were all human, once."

"You haven't answered my question, when and how were you made?" She sat the empty glass on the table. Without hesitation the door opened and JoAnne reappeared with a fresh drink.

"I think she's trying to get me drunk." After resting it in the spot the other vacated she actually curtsied and left.

Constantine uncrossed his legs and leaned forward, "You cannot get inebriated and I spoke with her about her mannerisms toward you. She agreed that you should be honored in an old-world way. I think it rather sporting of her."

"I think it's scary. When did you talk to her?"

"I can speak telepathically to her. You can command her to stop."

"How do I do that, telepathically? Can you read my mind?"

"You have a connection with her all you need do is want her to stop. I cannot read your mind. Not yet."

Rose rested her head back against the chair and let her mind drift back through some of the mother daughter moments she had shared with JoAnne. The way she sheltered Rose and catered to her every whim, the nighttime shopping trips and social gatherings. And that first vampire book the one JoAnne read over and over until Rose could read it from memory. That brought her attention back to Constantine. "Don't try to change the subject tell me how you were turned."

"Very well, I trapped a vampire forced him to drain me then I destroyed him."

"And you think I have an active imagination. No one seeks out a vampire let alone traps one." She chuckled but it faded when Constantine failed to smile. "You're not kidding, are you?"

"Why would I?" He sat as still as stone.

"How did you trap him and what did you do with him?"

"I bled myself and lay in wait. When the vampire approached and began to feed on me and my manservant harnessed him with chains made of the finest Spanish silver. He bled the vampire on my behalf until I was strong enough to feed directly from him. And feed I did, until there was not a single drop of immortal blood left in his body." His eyes danced with recollection, "Then I chained him to a stake as to allow the sun to destroy him. The next evening, when I awoke I scattered the ashes to the wind and buried the remainder of the skull under a bed of thorn roses."

Rose laughed, "A little over kill don't you think. How powerful could the vamp have been if you were able to capture him?"

Constantine slammed his fist on the table. The centerpiece jumped and settled several inches from its' original spot. He growled and leaned in close to her, "You call me a liar."

"No, I just think it was a little much. Wasn't the sun enough to destroy him?"

"Perhaps, but even in ashes a vampire can be reborn if the blood is powerful enough. I take no chances." Constantine returned his drink to the table and applauded. "I have not had such a pleasurable conversation in decades, thank you. I suppose you are anxious to get some air. It has been quite a while without a reprieve." He stood his hand extended to Rose. "Shall we?"

"I've not eaten."

"What would be to your delight?"

"A rare steak."

"And?"

"That's it."

The door opened and in stepped JoAnne with a domed platter.

As with a last meal, Rose savored every morsel of meat.

Constantine tapped his talon like nails against the ancient wood table. "You've eaten every morsel and your stomach has retained it quite nicely. Think of this as your last meal. Now let us depart."

As she stood Rose rested her fingers flat atop Constantine's waiting arm.

He escorted her to the darker side of the room to a door with a stain glass window in it. On the other side of the door a spiral staircase led upwards hundreds of feet. Constantine turned, faced Rose, then placed her hand on his shoulder wrapped his arm around her waist. He gave a fierce lunge up.

"Hold on."

The wind and the corkscrew motion made Rose dizzy. She couldn't watch as they approached the top so she buried her face deep into his chest. His solid and unyielding body still felt warm from his last feed. She clung tighter to him for fear of falling and felt his body respond. *Typical guy!*

A rush of cold air, a pop in her ears and they were free. Rose lifted her head to see an inky black sky punctured by a million sparkling stars. Looking down she realized they had flown hundreds of feet into the air above the mansion, the one Sonny James had purchased with her families' money. *I knew it! I was below ground.*

"I know you have never seen such a magnificent sight. When I have turned you, I will show you wondrous things that will astound you. You will see in a different way, with a clarity that is only vampire."

"So, you keep telling me, I can't wait." Rose sniped sarcastically.

Constantine placed a finger over her lips, "no need to shout my pet. We are the only two in the heavens tonight and I hear perfectly." He blessed her forehead with a kiss.

The darkness engulfed all noise. Her heart beat harder when she looked down and realized just how high they were. Below, the rooftops looked more like stones between groups of trees.

"There…" He pointed, "is your home." Ancient Oak trees lined the streets in a straight pattern. In the back yard, just below the terraced half, a row of wild thorn roses grew thick. Their brilliant and deep red color stood out among the mossy green grass.

I never noticed those.

"We will end our nightly journey there, later, so that we might begin our eternal adventure before sunrise." Constantine squeezed tighter around her waist while an unchecked smile grew across Rose's face.

"How high can you fly?" Rose felt a little queasy and thought conversation would help.

"As high as I like." He chuckled. "Would you like to go higher?" His voice resonated with challenge.

"Why not?"

With a jerk they were off. They climbed faster and higher than the sprinkling of clouds. The g-force began to contort her face. The air turned thin and the bright stars began to fade as Rose fought impending unconsciousness.

"It is so peaceful here. Rose?" The last words she heard before she fainted.

A free fall was not what she had in mind but as soon as they reached the lower altitude she came to quickly. Constantine found it so comical he laughed, "You waned, my dear and me without my vinegars. My apologies, I forget, until you have completely turned you cannot take the altitude the way I can."

They had plummeted several hundred feet in a matter of seconds. Rose held on so tight her fingers were still numb. Then she felt a sharp ping on her cheek. Capturing a piece of hair in her mouth she discovered ice on the tips. Constantine slowed their decent.

"Want to go once more?" He quizzed jokingly.

"No, I'm good. Once you've been there —" She shrugged.

"What would you like to see?"

Rose thought for several long moments, "Ground." Then she thought, "My mother's grave."

"Why, it is morbid, I love the idea."

"I can say my peace. I was interrupted by the paparazzi, before."

"How is it that I am incapable of denying you any request?"

"Let me go?"

"Ha! You still have your wits about you."

In a few moments they landed in the graveyard just steps from her mother's grave. The night was warm with a gentle breeze that gave Rose a chill that once again made her think of the old wives tale Jeremy had told her about stepping on ones' own grave. Standing next to her mother she pondered how it would feel to be dead. It seemed a lifetime since she first came to Atlanta. And now here she stood by the grave of the only blood relation she knew with a creature who's desire it was to make her his possession.

Rose fell to her knees. The flowers had since been removed grass grew up the front of the head stone. The words carved into it as hollow as Constantine's heart:

Mother, Daughter, Wife, Woman of God, Rest in Peace

"Oh, come now, there is no need to get the vapors I told you I am in short supply of vinegars." He placed his hand on Roses shoulder.

She jerked his hand away and fell forward, "Mother, I am so sorry. Please, forgive me."

"Alright, well done, let us leave this place. Death is so dreary and we have so much to do my patience is tested."

"Fine, I said what I wanted to." Rose stood and from the corner of her eye she spied something that moved among the trees. Constantine took no note so she dismissed it as being the caretaker but her eye caught a glimpse of the stone next to her mother's grave. The head stone read: ROSE ANNE BODIN

Rose gasped and fell backwards her hands over her mouth to muffle the scream. Constantine grabbed her arm and righted her on her feet. She turned with a look of horror and screamed aloud, "I'm not dead!"

"But you are dead to this world. You died in a tragic explosion at your cabin in Savannah. The gas equipment so old and rusty it was horrific timing to have gone off on the first night of your stay. And your publicist so young, tsk-tsk. JoAnne was to explain this."

Rose stepped away from the stone shaking her head at the surreal moment before her.

I'm really dead?

"Feel better?"

"No! What about my fans? Was there a funeral? Who came?"

"Everyone, you were loved my dear. And so tragic, several overly zealous fans actually committed suicide over your death. I do not understand the flood of emotions. I do not feel them. Even when I was human I did not. The dead are not entertaining."

"Like you?"

"I am undead, as a vampire you will be able to see all realms of beings as well as the dead ones."

"Will I be able to speak to my mother?" Rose wiped at tears.

"You may see her from time to time, if she chose to stay in this realm, but the dead have a different agenda they have no use for eternal creatures. Besides they are cryptic and never get to the point of the matter. I think it is jealousy that prevents them from interacting with us. Alas, it is of no consequence to me and should be of no consequence to you, you have bigger things to think about tonight. For instance, you will need to change your name. Perhaps."

"Change my name, why?"

"Rose Bodin is dead."

"You keep saying that, I—" Rose looked again at her head stone. No date just her name carved into black granite.

Constantine continued. "You need to establish a corporation that can support your wealth from century to century without causing suspicions. Something basic that can be handed down through generations. You will need JoAnne's help. She has attentively secured most of your holdings since she was the last living relative of record."

"She ordered the tombstone too?"

"Yes."

"Figures, let's go I've had enough."

Chapter Twenty

The lights of the big city captivated Rose. When they came to the darker side Constantine whispered in a low serious tone. "Now I will show you my side of the city."

The closer they got to the ground, dogs began to bark and howl. The street had a shimmer and the air still smelled of rain and wet dog.

"It must've rained?" Rose let go and stepped away from Constantine's grasp. She adjusted her clothes and looked around. The dogs quieted one by one. For a summer evening it felt ominously quiet and cooler. No kids out playing, not even a cricket or a night bird made a sound. The silence shattered with the shriek of a police siren. Lights flashed as a black and white patrol car passed at the end of the street.

Rose turned back toward Constantine but she was alone.

"Constantine?" Rose whispered in a harsh voice.

"Constantine, where the hell are you? You can't just leave me here?" Walking to the curb she observed a row of houses, if you could call them that. Square shacks with dilapidated porches but someone found them livable several had dim lights burning in the windows.

Run!

On the neglected sidewalk she tried to run north but stumbled several times on the uneven concrete. Heels and a silk evening gown were not the best attire for running so she removed the shoes and carried them. She set her sights toward the lights of the big city. Noises echoed off the empty streets camouflaging their origin; a woman screamed obscenities at a delinquent boyfriend, a bum sleeping by a tree held out his hand with a grunt. A wire-haired dog approached barking and snarling with his ears laid back and the tuft of hair at his rump standing on end but Rose looked him in the eye and growled; he tucked his tail and ran away with a yelp. *Wow, that really worked.*

Reaching a corner store by a crossroad she walked up to a pay phone that hung on the wall by the door. It was out of order, no cord. She stood for several seconds before she felt that cold chill up her spine.

"Constantine?" She shivered hard but not from being physically cold. A crack, a footstep, that wasn't Constantine, he never made a sound. Then out of the darkness a match was snapped to life, the smell of sulfur and then the pungent smoky odor of a cheap cigar billowed out of the darkness. Three men stepped into the glow of the neon signs pulsating through the store windows.

"You look like you just come from a party. Why was we not invited?" The shortest spoke first. His worn leather jacket hung past his fingertips. The man's nervous demeanor and the way he continued to glance at the other two prior to speaking indicated he was the lackey of the trio.

"I don't think she likes us? How come you don't like us?" This came from the fat one. His voice, creepily and unnaturally high pitched for a man. The alcohol emanating from their breath bridged the gap between them and became more acidic with each step they took towards her.

Rose stood her ground. Getting away from these guys wasn't an option in her heels or her stocking feet. *Constantine where the fuck are you?*

"What's your name pretty lady? And, why you wandering 'round my streets dressed in a costume?" This time it was the bald one, the one who had lit the cigar and now took a deep drag from it, who spoke. The lit tip of the cigar glowed deep red highlighting the meanness in the hoodlums' eyes.

"I'm lost." Rose tried to appear relaxed but she could feel a drop of sweat release from behind her ear and run down her neck.

The two flunkies approached while the bald one waited. Rose raised her finger and pointed at them, "I don't think you realize what you've gotten yourselves into."

Both men looked at each other and began laughing slapping each other on the back. One clearing of the throat from Baldy brought them to attention.

"Lady I don't think you know whose you talking to. 'Cause you 'bout to become one of T's hoes."

Both men turned serious then lunged toward her. Rose failed to move quickly enough and in moments the men had her in their grasp. Each held one of her arms by the wrist and elbow. She squirmed and jerked trying to get free but she wasn't strong enough. The Baldy approached looking very confident. He stood to her left side leaned in and slowly blew cigar smoke in her face. Rose coughed and spat. Her eyes began to tear.

"Don't cry, I'm gonna make you the happiest woman in 'lanta tonight." The bald man gestured and the other two pulled Rose hard against the wall.

"You're gonna regret this." Rose's voice was harsh and deeper than usual as her faith in Constantine waivered.

"No. Not tonight." He put the lit end of the cigar so close to her cheek the hair sizzled. Baldy grabbed her dress and pulled hard exposing her garter belt and hose.

The attackers face gleamed with excitement, "Did you wear this for me? I'm impressed but you won't need all the fancy dressin'." He slid his stubby fingers up between her legs. Rose recoiled and kicked. "Hold her steady, dammit!"

The men reinforced their grip.

"Constantine!" Rose screamed his name. Nothing no response she cried, "Where are you?"

"Lady ain't nobody gonna come to this part of town at night."

"Fuck you!" Rose growled and felt a little bit of a release from the fat one.

"Yes, you will, now shut her up!" Baldy grabbed her harder his fingers groping toward their prize.

Fatty put his free hand over her mouth and that's when Rose clamped down hard and deep on his nubby forefinger. The man screamed releasing her wrist. His other hand tried in vain to open her mouth hitting and slapping at her face till he drew blood from the corner of her lip. The wound on the man's finger began to bleed freely. Rose could taste the blood as tiny streams of it trickled down her throat. The taste began to change from metallic to sweet.

Fatty slapped her with an open hand across the face, which caused her to release the appendage. She spat out the blood leaving several streaks on her chin and her dress. Rose swung her fist hard at the man holding her other arm but missed scrapping her knuckles across the surface of the brick wall. She was so full of adrenaline and barely felt the pain that should have radiated through her. She screamed in anger.

Shorty refused to let go of the one arm. Baldy stepped in front of her, his arms flailing against her one free arm, trying to grab her wrist, his unzipped pants invited Rose so she kicked as hard as she could. The heel of her foot landed square. He sucked in all the air his lungs could hold, his face bulged turning a purplish blue, his eyes welled and he went to his knees with a jolt.

Then she heard the click. She looked up at the muzzle of a big shiny gun. Shorty held it flat in a gangster's way but his hands shook.

"I'm gonna cap your ass, bitch!" The sweat poured from his forehead and dripped from his nose. His golden grilled teeth glistened against the neon.

"T, you alright?" He looked back at his friend.

The man on the ground moaned, "Fuck no! Don't cap her. I want to take my time."

Fatty had his shirt off and was wrapping it around his bloody finger. The tattoos covering his chest and arms were of demons. Rose felt a strange tingling sensation from the pit of her stomach, at first, she felt it might be a delayed reaction to the blood she ingested from Fatty but then decided it wasn't really like a retch but a warmness that traveled to her limbs. She began to tingle like tiny bolts of electricity passing through her. She felt alive and ready for a fight. Her eyes could see more clearly, it wasn't as dark as it had been. Bright halos surrounded every source of light. She could feel the blood rushing through her veins strengthening her muscles. She felt invincible. She could smell their fear.

Shorty pushed the gun up under her chin hard, his body twitched with excitement as he wrapped his arm around her, "hee hee hee hee, T gonna show you what bein' a lady's all about. You gonna get yours."

Just then Rose felt an overpowering urge to bite his right ear. She had it in her mouth before the man could react. The gun bounced on the ground landing between her and Baldy who still struggled to get to his feet. Shorty screamed as a chunk of the ear released into Rose's mouth. She spat the ear to the ground and wiped at the blood drooling down her neck. Rose reacted to the man's screams with a punch to his gut. He flew backward several feet to the wall of the store. He landed with such force several of the outer bricks broke spraying mortar onto the man's back as he landed on the asphalt face first.

Rose stared, with her mouth agape. *How the hell did I do that?*

She looked at her fists, stunned, covered in blood. She saw that Baldy had made his way to the gun. Before he could get his stubby fingers on it, she was on top of him. They struggled for a moment when the fat guy joined in. He grabbed Rose by the back of the head, his hand full of hair, he lifted her into the air and back on two feet.

"Let's see how brave you are now?" He retrieved a switchblade from his pocket and engaged it.

Rose's eyes wide with fear saw something pass across the man's face, a shadow. "Constantine!" Rose screamed in a voice unfamiliar to her.

"Shut the fuck up!" The man's fist landed square against her temple sending a shock of pain through her head then he yanked the handful of hair hard enough to bring Rose to her knees.

Just as she felt the cold steel blade against the thin skin at her throat, she heard a gulp and felt a tug. The knife made a pinging sound as it hit the concrete. When she turned the man was gone. The bald man and the short guy were left looking upward toward the night sky. Rose clambered to her feet and tried to run but her legs felt like lead and all she could do was collapse back to the ground.

"You are magnificent." Rose heard the words whispered in her ear but no one was there just an icy chill that floated around her.

"Constantine?"

Baldy began to scream as his body was dragged across the concrete into the shadows of the trees behind the corner store. There appeared to be no one doing the pulling just the bald man grabbing at his throat like a wild beast about to be slaughtered.

Rose grinned at the thought. "Don't worry, Shorty, you're about to get yours."

Just then the man jumped to his feet still holding the bloody spot where his right ear had been and took off running toward the main road a block away. Within seconds the short man screamed and disappeared into the shadows.

Rose felt completely void of energy. She sat on the asphalt of the parking area for what felt like hours. She pondered why no cops had come after all that screaming.

"Survival of the fittest." Constantine stood in the glow of the neon lights. From this distance she could almost make out a grin on his face.

"Where the fuck have you been? Those thugs could've killed me." Rose stood dusting off her dress and wiggling her feet back into her shoes.

"I wanted you to experience the feed. And, you did beautifully. Not nearly enough to keep up your strength but I think perhaps you understand what just a small amount of blood can do. Just imagine the strength a complete feed would give you."

"A feed, that's what this was about? I'm not a vampire, I'm still human I could've been killed, you asshole." Rose pushed back her hair and began to walk toward the main road.

Constantine approached. He extended his hand Rose slapped it.

He grabbed her "you will not be human for long." Then they lifted off the ground and took to the sky.

After several minutes Rose asked, "Where to now, Disneyland?"

"Oh, your sarcasm will be a delightful distraction. Your anger will bring you no benefit you must let it go and embrace your destiny. Now, I will show you the more civilized and current way to hunt but not until you are properly attired."

They came to rest in an alley at the back door of a nightclub.

"We need to make ourselves more presentable. You have a little blood on your—" he gently used his thumb to wipe at the blood dried to her chin then with a seductive motion he licked his thumb clean. He retrieved a handkerchief from his inside jacket pocket and placed it up to a drippy outside faucet that dampened it enough to clean away the grime from Rose's cheek.

"How the hell did I bite that man's ear off? I don't have fangs." She probed her mouth with her tongue.

"Survival, we are all animals by nature. Do not think on it any more tonight allow us to enjoy the remainder of the evening."

Rose thought hard about how she'd felt when the blood made its' way into her body. She'd never felt like that before. It felt savage, before blood just made her sick to her stomach. Constantine adjusted his sleeves and then fluffed her disheveled hair.

"Stop it." Rose slapped his arm away and stepped back. "I'm not an infant who needs tending." A low growl emanated from her. Shocked she reeled back and jerked one hand over her mouth. But she shot Constantine a "go to hell" look as he chuckled.

He raised his hands in surrender.

A noise as JoAnne stepped out of the shadows. "The clothes you requested."

In her hand she held a Louis Vuitton hanging bag. She handed it off to Constantine and quietly disappeared back into the darkness.

Constantine smiled, "She is efficient if nothing else." He offered Rose his elbow and motioned for them to enter through the partially opened door. The music pounded with a wild beat. Strange sounds she had never heard before drew her in, not really instruments but noises and rhythms overlapping one another in a strange melodic way. She soon found her own heart racing to the beat as her cheeks began to flush. It felt hot and clammy the closer they got to the sound. A black velvet drapery hung over an entrance and guarding the entrance a heavy-set black man with gun barrel arms and no neck. When Constantine and Rose approached the man smiled and extended a hand. His smiling face and slightly slanted eyes gave away his condition.

"Hi Constantine."

"Good evening, Raul. How are you on this fine night?"

"Raul is a-o-k!" He said with an enthusiastic thumbs up.

"Good. Is it a packed house?"

"Yes, sir but no one gets passed me unless they suppose to."

"That is wonderful Raul. Now my friend and I would like to pass."

"'Course. You know you're good-to-go." Raul lifted the velvet drape and motioned for them to enter.

Holding Rose's hand Constantine looked back, "His simple mind protects us and that in turn protects him. We cannot enter a mind so pure of thought."

He led her past speakers the size of a '57 Cadillac. Ahead, the biggest dance floor she'd ever seen came to life with throngs of people moving in unison. Young people, old people they all danced in the same manner, hypnotized. They jumped up and down to the beat of the music some waving their arms in the air as if being taken over by a wholly spirit they couldn't see but felt simultaneously. You could not tell who was with who, no one coupled they just danced and looked around as if they didn't see anyone else in the room. Constantine led the way around the crowded floor to a staircase that led to the second floor. Once they had ascended they crossed a landing that followed the edge of the dance floor. Rose could see down a long corridor and every few yards a glass door. The doors were blacked out so you could not see in.

Constantine took Rose to the third door and placed his thumb over a black box. A blue light passed under his thumb and the door clicked open with a woosh sound. As soon as they stepped across the threshold the door closed behind them and the music outside dissipated. All was quiet inside the room and it felt cold enough to cause the skin on Rose's neck to prickle. It took several seconds for Rose's eyes to adjust to the darkness after the laser light show on the dance floor.

The room was decorated in an Arab's oasis style with flowing sheer fabric and velvet panel draperies. A large sofa lined the back wall. Ornate bejeweled pillows with long fringe lay strewn on the floor. A crystal chandelier with candles hung from the champagne-colored fabricated ceiling.

Constantine turned to Rose, "We can converse, eat or . . ." he smiled, "drink. You must change into a more suitable ensemble."

He motioned for her to sit. She obliged letting go a deep heavy sigh as her body relaxed into the overstuffed pillows around her.

"Would you care for some refreshment?" He sounded gentlemanly and sincere.

"Sure, a cabernet, oh and maybe some Ahi Tuna."

"Whatever your heart desires."

"Then let me go."

"Oh, come now, are you not having fun? I am thoroughly amused. If you knew you could not be hurt or that you could heal yourself, would you not want that?"

"No."

Constantine reached for Rose's hand and held it to up to the candle light, "Then where, pray tell, is the wound you sustained during your battle with those hoodlums?"

Rose stared at her hand not even a bruise.

Constantine touched her temple, "The punch you sustained has healed also. Darling, you are already changing and you cannot stop it."

"If I kill you before I change doesn't that cure me?"

He laughed hard, "That is lore and you know it. To kill me would simply end our connection but you would be left just as you are, not all vampire but not all human. Unless we complete the transformation, you will never have the strength to kill anything other than human. Once I have turned you, I will be your maker and always stronger than you."

"What if I drink the blood of someone older and stronger than you?"

"Perhaps, but alas you are not the fortunate one. There is no one older than me."

"You can't be the oldest vampire in existence."

"No. There are older ones in distant lands. We will have eternity to discuss that and other worthwhile subjects."

Rose laid her head back against the cushions on the sofa and took several deep breaths. A knock came at the door.

Constantine commanded, "Enter."

A young voluptuous red head entered the room wearing a see through silk sari with tiny gold bells dangling from the silken braided trim. Her hair flowed in a river of red about her shoulders. On a golden tray she carried the requested drink and food. She placed everything onto the small ottoman in front of Rose.

"Thank you." Rose smiled.

The red head turned her attention to Constantine, she placed herself directly in front of him, she smiled he nodded. The young girl knelt between his knees took her hair into one hand and moved it to one shoulder, bared her throat and lifted her body upward offering herself to him. He used his index finger to trace a line from behind her ear to her breast. The woman's body quivered but she didn't make a sound.

Constantine glanced at Rose, "now this is the civilized way to partake of sustenance." He lifted the girl's chin another inch into the air and licked her throat. He slowly bit deep into her flesh. A gentle moan escaped the girl but she didn't falter. Constantine with his back slightly arched appeared to be in a state of euphoria. As he suckled the willing victim his eyes turned deep crimson and then black. His hair glistened as he turned his head gently from side to side like a lover passionately kissing his beloved. A thin stream of blood began to flow from her neck down to her shoulder once there it reached a crevice that diverted the stream to her breast. The blood a stark contrast to the bright white skin pulsed and called to Rose.

I'm watching a vampire feed?

Rose stared unable to look away. Captivated by the girl's willingness she leaned closer. Her heart raced and her palms began to sweat. The vein in the volunteer victims neck pulsated just millimeters below the warm vital skin.

Rose felt her mouth go dry and drank the wine in several big gulps and took two bites of raw fish. Constantine pulled away leaving the girl even more pale than when she arrived. She waivered a little, stood, turned to Rose and asked, "If you would like I can show you to the powder room so you could freshen up?"

Rose stood. "Sounds good to me."

Constantine waved the two on then settled back on the pillows. They grabbed the dress bag and exited the room.

Once outside the door the tasty morsel spoke, "I'm Angelica if you need anything just ask." She leaned close her perfume smelled of lilac.

Smells better than Rebekah. "Angelica how old are you?"

"I'm twenty-three and a half."

"Why do you allow a vampire to drink your blood?"

"Better than hooking, the pay's better too. I use to sell my plasma to the blood bank this is about the same only better. I get a little high out of it."

"How much do you make?"

"I get paid by the club depending on the shift about thirty dollars an hour but then I get good tips from the vampires. The wampires don't tip as good, if they tip at all."

"Wampires, what are wampires?"

"You know, a vampire wanna be; a human who drinks blood, till they get sick, the dumb asses." Angelica laughed.

They entered an open archway at the end of the hall and passed through a heavy metal door to the bathroom. The décor was that of a Roman bath with mosaic tiles and columns and just inside the sitting area a smoky full-length mirror. Rose stopped and looked at her reflection. Hair a tangled mess and the shoes had black asphalt stains. Then there was the blood, smears and drops and splatters all over the lavender dress. The restroom was sound proof, no echoes. Rose adjusted her voice, "So what else do wampires do?"

"Oh, some have their teeth shaved to look like fangs and have their nails manicured, they bleach their skin or wear make-up to look even more-white, and shit like that." Angelica took a thick cloth from a basket and wet it with hot water. Ringing it out Rose noticed old bite marks on her wrist.

"How often do you get bit?"

"Our manager keeps track. There's a doctor on staff to check us out. It's more for them than us. They don't want us to give them bad blood." She rolled her eyes as she cleaned the wounds on her neck.

Rose stepped into the stall to change. She hung the bag from the hook on the backside of the door. She pushed the straps off her shoulders and the dress glided down her body to the floor. After close examination she realized there was not a mark on her, not a bruise or a scratch. She unsnapped the garter and let the tattered hose fall. She kicked them off then dropped them into the bin next to the toilet. Rose ran her hands over her tummy, the skin goosed bumped and tingled. Her tummy growled a little as it digested the meat from earlier. *I am human.*

She unzipped the bag to examine what JoAnne had brought her to wear, on the hanger her favorite brand of jeans and a Dallas Cowboys sweatshirt and a black camisole, in the bottom of the bag a pair of sneakers. "Thank you, JoAnne."

"What?" Angelica was at the door.

"Oh, nothing I'll be out in a sec." Rose peed, *that's human.* She flushed.

"I can help you with your hair. I use to be a hairdresser, back in the day." Rose exited the stall, Angelica whistled, "You'll knock 'em dead honey."

"I wish." Rose washed her hands and neck with hot water and soap.

Angelica began to brush Rose's hair, "Wow, your skin is off the hook. I mean it's clear and not even a wrinkle. What do you use?"

"I don't use anything."

"No way. You gotta use moisturizer or something." Angelica reached out to touch Rose's cheek. Rose slapped her hand away.

"Sor-ry." Angelica continued to brush Rose's hair.

"Where's the exit? Can I get out from here?"

"You think I'd just let you leave. Constantine would kill me, hun." Angelica put her hand on Rose's shoulder. Rose spun around grabbing the girls' wrist and pinning her to the wall with one fell swoop. The girls' eyes widened with fear and her lips trembled, "Sorry, you can whoop my ass bloody but I'm more scared of him." Her eyes looked up and her eyebrows lifted.

Rose turned sharp her hand still on the girl, and there in the archway stood Constantine. He had changed his clothes. Now he wore a pair of black slacks, an ecru collarless shirt and a black silk jacket. He screamed GQ with a glint of monster.

"I wondered what could possibly be taking so much time and now I see, you ladies are getting acquainted, how sweet. Rose, you will join me back in our suite, now." He turned.

She released the girl with a huff and followed Constantine out of the restroom.

Behind her Rose heard the girl tort, "Thanks for the tip!"

Rose froze in the doorway turned and glared at the waitress, "Don't run with scissors."

Chapter Twenty-One

Constantine appeared comfortable on the sofa and let out a sigh his breath both sweet and putrid, filled the room. Rose shivered.

Constantine motioned to her, "By all means eat more. You will need your strength." He laid his head back against the cushions and began to breathe in a quick shallow way like a newborn kitten after it's gorged on mothers' milk.

Rose looked at the food on the platter and felt nauseous. She watched for several more minutes as Constantine rested.

Run! She felt the urge but new better than to make any sudden movements so she stood slowly keeping her eyes on her sleeping captor she inched her way to the door. The metal handle felt cold, the air around her thick. On the other side of the door the lights pulsed.

Where do I go? She thought twice about running and turned. The scream escaped her throat before she had time to stop it. Constantine was on her. Rose backed against the door to give herself a few inches separation from him and he closed in with a whisper. He pinned her to the door without physically touching her. Sweat beaded her upper lip an urge to lick her lips made her tremble.

Constantine inhaled deeply, "You are mine but that alone will not stop another vampire from devouring you. This is not a safe place for one so young to wander."

"So why did you bring me here?" Rose's tone spiked with anger.

Cold flesh touched her ear. "I like it here."

Rose felt her body lift and without warning she sailed through the air and landed hard on the sofa cushions, her head bounced several times causing her to bite her lip. Constantine was on her before she could attempt to rise. Rose tasted the blood oozing from her bottom lip.

"Turn me! Kill me! Eat me! Do what the fuck you're gonna do but dammit do it!"

"So histrionic." He leaned in closer and licked the smear of blood on her lip with a rough and icy tongue. His body trembled and he quickly moved away from her. "I will decide when the time is right." He pulled at his cuffs.

"When will that be?"

"You will know."

"When?" Rose was up and making her way toward Constantine. "When?"

He grabbed her by the arms and lifted her into the air he held her tight and brought her firmly against him. Rose could feel the power in him cresting. He brought his arms around her, his hands now on each cheek of her buttocks. He pressed her harder against his body. She could feel a throbbing in his crotch.

"You're warm again."

"Warm enough to be your lover?" He kissed her hard his lips cold his tongue sharp as he plunged into her mouth then licked at her lips. Rose struggle to get free but it was useless. She moaned when she felt her nipples tighten and her female parts quiver. The last thing she wanted was to have her body respond in this way. It was another betrayal, an indignation that she had no control over. She whimpered at the thought of sex with this narcissistic tick. Or were all vampires like Constantine? She let her body go limp.

"Let me go." He let her go. Her body crumpled to the carpet like a pile of dirty laundry. She buried her face in her hands.

"You can no longer exist in that world. You must accept that you are destined to be immortal with me." He stepped over her and sat on the jeweled chair, a king on his throne.

"I choose my own destiny. And, I choose to stay human!" Rose shouted with tears pouring down her cheeks her fists in the air.

"It is too late for that."

Chapter Twenty-Two

Nothing was said between them for at least an hour until Constantine stood, "It is time to go."

He grabbed her by the arm and lifted her to his side. They were out of the club within seconds. The cool air outside felt great as Rose took several deep and cleansing breaths. "Where are we going? I'm tired."

"To see someone who may enlighten you and give you a different perspective."

Rose recognized the place immediately, the Crimson Café. The lone bulb shone on the alley behind the building casting wicked shadows as they approached. The door opened easily without fanfare or a key. Inside Rose got the same sensation as before musty and dank. They made their way through the darkened café to the bar. Constantine took down the bottle of Grand Marnier and put it on the bar in front of Rose.

"I'm becoming an alcoholic." She opened the bottle and put the spout to her lips and drank. It burned going down at first but then quickly became refreshing.

"Alcohol does not affect the vampire body the way it does human. You could drink your weight in alcohol and it will not inebriate. Have your fill for soon you will only crave blood."

The place on her lip that she had bit earlier had already healed. Rose ran her tongue over her lips and a shudder ran through her. *I must be changing.*

A noise, she flinched. Constantine pulled the bookcase away from the wall. It turned on an axis to expose a dark hole behind. "Come."

"Why?" She was already off the bar stool and headed toward him. "Never mind, I know, I will see." She waved her hands in the air in a shivering motion and walked into the darkness.

The dirt surface felt cool to the touch and the dank air clung to her tiny nose hairs evoking a sudden and violent sneeze. "Aha! Vampires don't sneeze." Rose wiped at her nose.

Constantine chuckled, "Vampires do not sneeze, Gesundheit!"

Rose heard a growl that raised the hair on her skin and elicited an urge to pee herself.

She grabbed Constantine's arm and whispered, "What the fuck was that?"

He put his finger to her lips and shushed her. Constantine called out, "Rebekah."

"Why didn't you say so, come on down." Her voice as melodic and sweet as the perfume she wore.

At the end of the dirt staircase a wooden door with steel hinges sat ajar. Flickering light emanated from around the edges of the door. Constantine used one finger to push it open and motioned for Rose to enter first. The warmth of the room wrapped around Rose like an electric blanket set on high. Goosebumps formed across her arms as her cooler skin adjusted. The floor, made of well-worn cobblestone had deep pile rugs strewn about. Furniture of another era, the civil war, maybe, decorated every inch of the candle lit room. In one corner a curtain drew back to expose Rebekah dressed in a white long-sleeved gown with a blue sash tied tight. Her hair braided into one thick strand lay across one shoulder. The scene almost worked except for the slight smear of blood above her lip. Rose's eyes widened at the realization that Rebekah was a vampire.

Rebekah reached out her arms and approached quickly then took a step back and looked deep into Rose's eyes, "You haven't turned yet? I'm sorry, you really should, its' grand." She wrapped her arms around Rose, nearly squeezed the breath from her lungs.

"Come have a seat, we'll talk for a while." Rebekah led Rose to the red velvet settee.

"Would you like some tea?" Rebekah reached for a painted porcelain pot on a tray.

Rose shook her head and motioned at the blood smear. Rebekah nodded, "Thank you, how rude of me." She wiped at her lips with a napkin then poured steaming liquid into two dainty teacups.

"So, what do you think of my humble abode?"

"Very nice. A little dated, but cozy." Rose took in the aged details. The tattered and thin draperies on the wall to mimic a window seemed less macabre than desperate.

"It's an old slave tunnel I discovered under the hat store. These tunnels lay under the city in a maze of routes. You've been to Underground Atlanta?"

Rose answered with a nod when a deep moan from behind the curtain drew everyone's attention. Rebekah looked around nervously, grabbed her napkin and stood twisting it in her hands. Rose gasped as Jeremy appeared, shirtless his jeans unbuckled his skin pale and ruddy. Sweat beaded around his neck and chest then his eyes flew open wide.

"Oh, wow, caught with my pants down." He tugged at the unzipped jeans and turned.

Rose stood as the cup she held left her grip and smashed to the ground, "What the hell are you doing here? They're vampires!"

"I know. But who can resist those big brown eyes and the unbelievable high from their blood, not me. I thought you of all people would understand."

"Understand what, that you're whoring yourself to a vampire that shouldn't even exist. I understand you're a meal to her and nothing more."

Rose grabbed him by the wrist and without thinking, "We're leaving!"

She walked the several dozen feet to the door, Jeremy in tow, but Constantine was already there. Rose glared, determined to have her way, "Get out of my way. He's just a boy, he doesn't understand! He should be allowed to leave before—" She dropped her head as the reality of the situation grabbed her mind. Neither of them would ever leave.

Jeremy pulled away and walked back to Rebekah. "This is where I want to be. I love her and I want to spend eternity with her."

"You don't know what you're talking about. She'll never turn you and if she does, it'll be too late, too late to ever go back." She plopped down on an overstuffed ottoman with her head in her hands.

Rebekah wrapped her hand around Jeremy's arm. Looking back at Constantine she took on a serious tone, "You'd better turn her soon or you may lose her." Rebekah and Jeremy disappeared behind the drapery and into the darkness of the tunnels that lay beyond.

Constantine held out his hand to Rose, "that was awkward. Let us depart to a more cheerful endeavor." She looked up. The shock in Constantine's eyes told her something was wrong. Rose wiped at the tears on her cheeks. There was blood!

"Oh God no!"

"Come now, it is a beautiful sight. Do not despair it is only the beginning we have a long way to go." He lifted her up and into his arms and carried her back up to the café.

Standing in the alley Constantine removed a lace handkerchief from his sleeve and handed it to Rose. She wiped at the bloody tear-stained tracks as though they were contagious.

"I'm tired; I want to get it over with."

"Soon enough, my love." Constantine took Rose's hand in his and they began to walk.

The night air was cooler now and Rose could feel Constantine's flesh cooling as well.

"How long do you stay warm after a feed?" She kept her eyes ahead of her, not wanting to see the smirk she could feel spreading across his face. If she was destined to become a vampire, she had to learn all she could before it happened. She needed to separate fact from fiction.

"That would depend on the amount of blood I consumed. If a mature vampire like myself were to desire a human like body temperature it would take at least two adults and the effect could last as long as a night. But the temperature is irrelevant to the satiation factor. I can go a week between feedings if I have fed sufficiently. It is the hunt that is most intoxicating."

"You like playing with your food?"

"Obviously." He gently squeezed her hand.

"I'm not just food though, am I?"

"No, my darling, you are much more than sustenance. Else I would have devoured you as a child. You are a different kind of food. You feed my mind and my spirit."

"You don't have a spirit!"

Chapter Twenty-Three

Bells began to toll. The sound echoed throughout the city.

"In a manner of speaking, it is my spirit of nature I refer to. I am a hunter and challenging prey is difficult to come by. After centuries of searching, I found you."

Rose tried to pull her hand away but Constantine tightened his grip. He continued to walk in a slow steady pace. They had been walking for what felt like hours but the bells declared it was only midnight.

Bells, church!

"What church bells are ringing?"

Constantine continued, "St. Luke's. Thinking about claiming sanctuary?" He chuckled. "That is only a fairy tale. I can walk on sacred ground I can kneel before an altar, if I so choose, without harm. Can you?"

"What do you mean?"

"Supplication is for the weak and simple minded. You are not weak or simple minded."

Rose did not answer so he went on, "Religion is a vice designed to squeeze wealth and submission from the common folk. It has brought about the destruction of kings, the annihilation of civilizations and is used to cloak the truth."

"The truth about what?"

"Me. What do you think would happen to society if it were widely known that vampires exist?"

"Chaos."

"The church has power because people willingly sacrifice their own and accept what it is that they are taught by those who have enormous power. There is nothing magical about the church or the things that are in it. It will not harm you once you have turned and you cannot harm me."

"What kills vampires? I need to know what to avoid, right?"

"Sunlight, it is pure and powerful. Silver, holy water, thorn roses they are meant to restrain, they alone do not destroy. And they must be of pure quality. Most of these you already know because of your writings. The rest I will teach you after."

"What about a stake through the heart?" Rose placed her palm against her chest.

Still there. She sighed heavily with the thump of her own heartbeat.

"It alone does not kill it brings about discomfort." He paused for a moment, "Although, for one as young as you, you may not be capable of recovering from a complete loss of blood, best to avoid stakes to the heart."

"I'll keep that in mind. What about slayers?"

"You are very inquisitive it is a nice change. Slayers are as old as vampires. They customarily hand down their skills and weapons to worthy family members who demonstrate a penchant for the work. But alas it has been many generations since I last came face to face with a true slayer."

"So, I have nothing to fear?"

"I believe you are safe." He lifted her hand to his thin lips he kissed it then turned and licked her wrist with a quick flash of his tongue.

Rose shivered violently in response. She wanted desperately to wipe her wrist but he held it tight by his side.

They continued to walk down Peachtree Street in the wee hours of the night. The air hung thick with the blossoming Magnolia, Dogwood and Pine trees. Distant trains whistled and moaned sadly while on occasion the night split with red and blue police lights and sirens. Rose silently prayed for someone to see them and to realize she needed to be rescued from the evil monster that held her hand.

"Where are we going now?" Rose squeezed his hand and firmly pulled hers away.

"A stroll through the park would be most pleasant."

"I don't think so!" Rose took off running in the direction of the church bells.

He'll catch me but I gotta try! Her mind raced as she ran. Faster than she'd ever run in her life she was at the church in moments. *Getting faster!* She tried the front door, locked. She ran around the back into a small courtyard. There were several dogwood trees, and one giant pine in the center. Several benches sat waiting for an occupant. There were no less than five different doors around the building.

No time to try them all. The tower! No, I'll be trapped. The kitchen? The sanctuary?

Rose heard a click. A door opened a bit and a hand motioned for her to enter. Rose looked around and entered the door. It was pitch black but she could hear a familiar heavy breathing.

"Dwayne? Is that you?"

"Yeah, sssshhhhh." He spit a little onto Rose's cheek. She wiped at it, he grabbed her hand. "Follow me."

She did as she was told without saying a word. They entered another door and the chilled musty smell told her they were headed underground.

Again?

They went down further and further under the church. Dwayne stopped, retrieved a box of wooden matches from his pocket. He shook them, retrieved one and struck it. The smell of sulfur stung her nose and drifted down the back of her throat until she could taste it. He lit a lantern on the wall. Before them another door, only this one was heavily chained and needed a key. Dwayne lifted a thick set, on a dark rusty ring, from his belt. It opened without difficulty. Dwayne pushed the door and pulled Rose through.

Inside felt like outside, open and fresh, not musty as it had been under the cafe. Rose took in a deep cleansing breath. *No Magnolia.*

She could hear water trickling. Then a burst of light as Dwayne flipped a switch. Rose caught her breath, Dwayne caught her. She had taken a step back and almost off the landing. Looking around Rose could see they stood at the top of a staircase several hundred feet above the floor inside a cavern. Dwayne took Rose's hand and led her down the winding stone steps to the bottom. The giant underground cavern was cut in half by a natural spring and a waterfall. The water falling created a gentle breeze that blew across and upward, swinging Rose's hair around her shoulders. Some of the walls donned thick layers of dark green moss while others glistened with thin clear streams of water that disappeared into cracks at the base. Across from the entrance another door waited. Dwayne walked fast once they reached the floor. He looked back at Rose several times and giggled. Dwayne used another key to open the last door. A small chapel lay beyond.

"I'm not a Catholic but I know that doesn't look like the Virgin Mary?" She pointed to a painting of a woman and baby.

"Not." Dwayne answered, shook his head and went about setting up the pulpit, lighting candles and arranging books.

"What are we doing here? What is this place?"

"You got boogey man. This safe place." He smiled so innocently, happily. His eyes lit the way to his soul, as pure as the water that ran through the middle of the place.

"Yes, I have a boogey man. And I need to get rid of him."

"Dwayne know." He pointed to the book he had placed on the pulpit.

"What's that?"

"Don't read good. Yeah, yeah, you read." Dwayne nudged her toward the altar.

"Okay." Rose stepped up the two steps to the pulpit and looked at the open pages. The images that stared back at her made her entire body go weak. The colorful impressions were of people surrounding a vampire on fire at sunrise. These were ancient people, Roman, maybe. Those that weren't naked wore tunics and carried rocks, sharpened sticks and blades. The book was written in an old language of Latin or Italian nothing Rose could understand. She flipped to the cover and on the front, carved into the leather, a depiction of an old tree with roots deep in the ground and on the very tip of the tiniest scraggly branch one drop of blood. It sent shivers of recognition through her body as goose bumps formed on her neck down her arms to the fingers caressing the book. A tiny spark forced a jerked release of the book.

"I can't read this it's in Latin or something." Rose slapped the book.

Dwayne huffed, and turned to the back of the book where several pages were written with a more legible script in English.

"Oh, okay, that's better." Rose studied the words.

She read silently to herself until Dwayne's voice startled her into reading aloud, "And they chased the abomination from the cavern into the sunlight where God cast fire upon the wretched creature burning it to ashes which he then scattered on the winds. And on that site shall the chosen one learn her fate and duty to her family and humanity." Rose looked up. *This is not real.*

"Dwayne, what does this mean?" Rose knitted her eyebrows in disbelief.

"You kill boogey man. Only girls kill boogey man."

"How? Run him into the sunlight? I don't think he'll go willingly."

Dwayne laughed.

"Dwayne, how do you know about this place?" Rose closed the book.

Dwayne announced, "Rose kill boogey man. You 'member?" Then he applauded.

"Dwayne, I kill Constantine?" *Oh, God, I'm talking like him.*

"Yeah."

"How do you know?"

"Grannie teach us, you and me. Dwayne can't kill. Rose can."

"Okay. Grannie, taught me how to kill Constantine? So how do I kill him if I don't remember?"

Dwayne pointed. "Rose kill boogey man, use knife."

"Okay, Dwayne. I'll kill the boogey man, but it's gonna take a hell of a lot more than just a knife."

Dwayne clapped his hands vigorously and grinned wide enough to pop his ears off then he pointed to a chest at the end of the first pew.

Rose approached the small wooden chest covered with broken, rusted metal locks. She lifted the creaky lid and peered inside. There were old knives and other things like books and pieces of cloth with fur, crosses and bottles of clear liquids. I hope that's holy water, she thought.

Something caught her attention, a photograph. A black and white picture of her with her grandmother and mother in this place by the altar and on the back of the photo written in ink, *another Rose blooms.*

"This must've been taken just days before my family died. I look the same as I did in the one on Sonny's mantel. Dwayne, do you know when this was taken?"

"That day, Rose chosen." Dwayne had a distant look in his eyes.

"Dwayne, what are you talking about? Rose chosen." She had to pull his face to hers to get his attention.

He blinked and pointed to the book. "Rose next slayer."

Rose went back to the book. She leafed through the pages until she saw a family tree with her name on it. A history of her family and beside certain names in red ink, a mark, a dagger. Her name, her mother's name and her grandmothers' name all had a dagger by them. At the bottom of the page, *let it be known to all that the chosen one is Rose.*

A slayer! No fucking way! She was already part vampire how could she be a slayer? And, who the hell said so?

A rumbling from above stole their attention. Dwayne looked up, "Go!"

Rose ran from the small sanctuary across the cavern and up the stairs back to the heavy door. She turned back to see Dwayne shutting the door of the room. He waved her on and she left.

Back outside she heard a terrible ruckus coming from inside the church. She made her way into the main body of the church. There at the altar Constantine stood with his head reared back in a horribly contorted way. The flickering of the candles cast an evil shadow about his form as he growled with his fist in the air. He lifted his nose and inhaled deeply. He turned slowly, calculatedly toward Rose. A moan grew from deep inside him and methodically made its way to his mouth which he then released.

He leaped to within inches of her face, his breath hard and deliberate his lip trembled as it curled back exposing his extended fangs. "I've missed you." He hissed.

He pressed his body against hers hard pushing her into the altar rail. His lips engulfed hers he wrapped his arms around her waist as he drove his rancid tongue deep into her mouth. She lifted her arms above his head then ran her fingers down his back. He responded as a man would. He lifted her almost a foot off the floor and pressed himself harder against her, she moaned. She didn't try to get free, now wasn't the time.

"I missed you." She answered with baited breath. He pressed harder she couldn't get enough air back into her lungs to complete her next inhale.

"You have been naughty. You are learning to enjoy your speed and agility. Now you can learn how to use your sexual prowess. Make me believe you want me or die here among the relics."

Rose went limp. "I'd rather be dead."

Just then the door behind them flew open with a loud echoing bang. Dwayne shouted, "Go boogey man!"

"We have out stayed our welcome." Constantine took Rose by the hand placed her solidly on her feet, turned, hissed at Dwayne and charged the aisle.

Without a sliver of fear Dwayne laughed.

Constantine, Rose in tow, made his way back out into the night but Rose took one last glance back at the church to see Dwayne still standing on the steps, waving goodbye with a big grin on his face.

Rose thought about how unreal it felt to know she could be a descendant of slayers. With all that had transpired between her and Constantine why didn't he see it? *Is he blinded by his lust for me? Could I really summon some ancient courage in order to kill him? Did a knife or dagger exist that would kill him and if so, could I find it before it's too late?*

Chapter Twenty-Four

Rose, deep in thought, had not noticed where they were headed until she smelled something familiar, Magnolia. She looked up as a blur whipped past her. Her hair flicked on the tail end of the wisp as cold flesh lapped her cheek. Rose spun on her heels in the direction of the wind. "What was that?"

Constantine's eyes flared with red and his fangs flashed white. He looked anxiously in all directions then sniffed deep at the air but with a cautiousness that brought the hair on the nape of Rose's neck on ends.

Constantine commanded in a gentle tone. "Detour."

"Okay, but—" Rose sucked in the rest of her words as Constantine yanked her so hard her feet lifted from the sidewalk. Constantine ran so fast her feet dangled, block after block, till they came to the Omni Hotel. After breathing in a huge gulp of air Rose exhaled, "Why are we here?"

"Because I desire to be here." He shook his head and it reverberated throughout his entire body like a dog shaking off excess water. "Now you will learn to be invisible in a public place."

"I already know how to do that." Rose dusted herself off and entered the turn-style doors without so much as a disruption of air. She glided quietly and unnoticed by the concierge and the front desk clerk, even the janitor dutifully mopping the floor failed to look up. She turned to Constantine and cocked her head to one side, snapped her fingers in the air above her head, she mouthed, "magic."

Constantine was beside her in a breath. He whispered on her neck, "You excite me beyond comprehension. We are to make the most fabulous couple of all eternity. Come."

Using a key fob Constantine pressed the penthouse floor button. Upon entering the vast marbled foyer the lights dimmed to a perfect setting, music began to play and the draperies opened in a silent wave of silken fabric. The night glowed brilliant. The bright lights of the city competed with the night sky winning favor over the sprinkling of stars that dusted the darkness in the distance. Every detail modern and fashionable from the leather furnishings to the enormous flat screen that appeared to be hung in the air above a gas lit fireplace with red glass stones already a glow. The room felt cold, as cold as Constantine, it was definitely his lair. "How many lairs do you have?" Rose shivered.

"Countless." He waved his hand the thought too trivial of a matter for him to contemplate.

Rose eyed an armchair with a blanket tossed over the back she settled in and wrapped the blanket around her. On the coffee table sat a copy of her last book. She picked it up and turned it over to the photo of her on the back. She looked so happy. How did she get to this point, about to be turned into a vampire by her own character? And, if it were truly possible, could she be a slayer? It was too much so she tossed the book aside.

"Not up for reading tonight?" Constantine smirked.

"What happened on the street tonight? What was that thing that passed by me? I felt it, I know something was there and it obviously startled you."

"I explained earlier that one as special as you who has the potential to entice jealousy among others of my kind. I must be more diligent until the process is complete and we are as one."

"I did see something earlier at the graves, didn't I. I knew I saw something move among the trees. So, another vamp is giving you the willies. That's funny."

"It would not be so humorous if he were to take you from me. He would then simply devour your blood and be done with you. Whereas, I want to give you the gift of eternal life."

"I don't want that gift."

A knock on the door brought Constantine to his feet. He looked to Rose and then to the door several times before a second knock demanded attention.

Rose smiled, "I think it's for you no one knows I'm here."

Constantine materialized at the door before the third knock. His hand trembled as it reached for the handle. It turned and the door flew open. A gust of wind blew into the room so fast it took Rose's breath. In an instant, she was face to face with a coldness she had never felt before. Constantine was cold but this was positively Arctic. She pulled the blanket up around her ears and shivered. Constantine flew to her side. She brought her knees up to her chest but something grabbed her ankles and yanked her free from the chair and the blanket. Her head just grazed the carpet. As her body was catapulted upward she could feel someone grab her under her arms and then place her firmly on her feet. She peered into the brightest bluest eyes she'd ever seen. She felt what breath she had left in her lungs escape her open mouth and her body went limp. Her right hand impulsively reached out for the angelic face before her. The white glowing skin, golden eyelashes, bright blue eyes and blonde/white hair were an impossible combination and she felt that if she refused to touch the skin, she would lose all sanity. The creature didn't flinch when her fingers rested on the crystalline cheek. She allowed her middle finger to brush over the thin pale lips, she made note that no breath came from the narrow nostrils. Then slowly as she felt her gaze being drawn to them, the lips began to part, first red flesh and then the flash of brilliant white fangs. Rose let go a scream only to be interrupted by Constantine as he grabbed her from the grasp of the golden creature.

They stood by the sliding door Constantine looked scared, his grip on Rose tighter than ever. *He's gonna jump!*

Rose looked up at him and let her eyes scream, 'JUMP!'

Within a millisecond they were padding across the street and back alleys.

With a whoosh of wind, they stopped at a clearing near a creek. Constantine released Rose and sniffed the air.

"Where are we now?" Rose trembled so hard the words bounced out of her mouth.

"We are now at Grant Park. We need to divert his attention."

"That was another vampire, and he wanted me?"

"Yes, but I will never surrender you. You are mine and once we have successfully escaped his blood lust we will get on with our exchange."

Glass shattered in the near distance and a roar of laughter filled the park then a familiar vibrato from a Harley kicked to life. Constantine smiled, "I have an idea. Wait here. Do not move."

"Yeah, whatever."

In a moment Constantine returned with a woman under his arm. She was clad in a fringed jacket with black leather riding chaps. Her nose, eyebrow and lip pierced, her left arm dark with tattoos. She giggled uncontrollably. "That was fucking hot! Do it again."

"Constantine, what are you planning?"

He pulled the woman towards Rose and forced them together. He pushed their faces cheek to cheek then tasseled their hair and ran his hands up and down their bodies. The woman wrapped an arm around Rose's neck. She put her nose to her ear, "I like girls too," she whispered.

"This is wicked. Can I get my old man to join us? He won't do the guy but he'll like you honey, you're sweet." As she leaned in to kiss Rose, Constantine separated them slashed a superficial cut to the girls' throat.

Rose looked at him confused. The woman put her hands on the wound, "Hey, what the fuck. I thought we were gonna have some fun, you said I'd have the time of my—"

Her words cut short by a white flash that snatched her up and flew towards the gazebo several hundred yards away.

Constantine pulled Rose by the arm, "Come we must leave here now. She will not appease him for long."

"You sacrificed her?"

"I delivered your scent to her so as to divert his attention from you. Trust me it is a bit of a ruse and will not last long, we must go now." Constantine forced her to run. When she couldn't keep up, he lifted her off the ground and carried her. Within minutes they were back at the Crimson Café.

"Wow, Constantine I've never seen you so agitated. I thought you were the baddest of the bad." Rose chuckled.

A growl reverberated from deep inside the vampire, "I am not afraid but I am not stupid and I will not allow anyone to get you. You are mine." In a blink Constantine had the shelves open and had disappeared into the tunnel.

"No thank you I'll just stay here." She placed her hand on the front door handle and before she could push it Constantine had her by the throat. He spun her around pressing her back against the door he then pressed himself against her.

He sniffed her neck and placed his lips lightly on her ear, "If you try that again I will let him have what is left of you. Remember, you are still human and right now that makes you prey." He took her wrist in his icy grip and pulled her to the tunnel. She could hear Rebekah arguing with Jeremy. By the time she got into the living area they were fully engaged in a yelling match. It was evident that she wanted him to leave in case things got bad with this other vamp but Jeremy, always the southern gentleman, was having none of it.

"You are human you can't fight him. It'll be hard enough for me and Constantine to fend him off." Rebekah pleaded.

"Not if you turn me now. I could take him. Think about it three against one. I like those odds better. Don't make me run like a coward, I'm no coward." Jeremy gave his best pout face.

"I know you aren't but I like you breathing and warm." Rebekah made a purring noise placed her open palm against his bare chest and things got quiet.

Rose looked to Constantine, "So what's the plan. She gonna turn him, you turn me and we try to fight this fang guy?" She could hear cooing and smacking from the other room.

Constantine paced and after what felt like an hour, "A newly turned vampire couldn't fight off anything. They need to feed and it would take hours and lots of human blood to build the kind of strength we need to fight a vampire like Phineas. No, we should not fight him. There are other ways. I just need to think."

Rebekah came from behind the curtain she had tears and blood smeared on her face. Her eyelids hung heavy with burden. She plopped onto the velvet chair and covered her face with her hands. "I didn't want this. Constantine why the hell would you come here if Phineas was after her? What were you thinking? Oh, I know, about yourself that is all you think about."

The realization hit Rose and she lunged for Rebekah, "You fucking bitch, you bit him. How could you he was just a boy?"

Constantine appeared between them before Rose could make contact but Rebekah didn't flinch, she would have allowed whatever punishment Rose wanted to dole out.

"I'm sorry, I tried to turn him but I guess he couldn't get enough of my blood fast enough, I don't know. I thought if I turned him Phineas would have no interest in a newbie vampire. I tried, I really tried." She broke into sobs.

Constantine put his hand on her shoulder, "Perhaps we can use this to our benefit." Rebekah screeched, "What are you talking about? My familiar, my love is dead by my hand because of your selfishness. I don't give a shit what Phineas does to you, me or your fucking human whore." Rebekah headed toward the door.

Rose took several steps toward Rebekah, "I am not a whore you blood lusting parasite bitch!"

Just then a rush of cold air entered the room, next a thud. All went eerily silent. Rebekah turned to face Rose a look of terror on her face and a hole where her throat had been. Blood pulsed and gushed down her chest. She went to her knees and then fell face first onto the pretty floral carpet, which promptly turned dark red as blood continued to pour from Rebekah's gaping wound. Constantine hissed and grabbed Rose. He tore through the curtain, passed the bed where Jeremy lay in a pool of blood. Rose made a mental note Jeremy had a peaceful almost contented look on his face like he died in his sleep with happy thoughts.

It suddenly got very dark. Rose could feel Constantine's arms around her but couldn't see him. The damp earth smell got stronger. *Great we're in the tunnels again.*

As Constantine ran with Rose in tow, she could hear various growls and screeches from behind them that at times felt on top of them. Rose took comfort in the fact she couldn't see a thing, it would probably be too horrific. *This is definitely going in the book.*

Constantine stopped abruptly. He put Rose onto her feet. He hadn't even broken a sweat and they'd been running for the good part of an hour. Constantine broke the silence, "I think he gave up. It is almost sunrise and I need to get to a lair. Follow me, we are not far from home."

"Home? Really, my home is a condo in Dallas, not some ancient southern Tara filled with vampires. You can go to hell I've had enough of this bullshit!" She turned and walked. The further she got the faster her pace became. She wondered at what point Constantine would pounce but he didn't so she just kept moving. The tunnels were well constructed and after a couple hours of walking she found herself back at Rebekah's. Jeremy and Rebekah were both gone and the blood had been cleaned. Rose laid down on the settee and covered up with an afghan laid over the pillows, without a thought as to who had cleaned the scene.

I don't want to cry. I might get blood on the pillow.

Wow, Rose Bodin famous vampire author turned vampire slash slayer who would have imagined that. She let her mind drift over the recent events and weighed her options.

If I walk out into the street and the sun is up I might burn. No one would believe me if I didn't burn, I would end up like my mother, Elizabeth, in an asylum/grave. I can't do this I have to keep up my strength so that I can find a way out of this. 'Rose - vampire slayer' that would make a great book, huh?

Her eyes heavy she drifted off to sleep with dreams of slaying old world vampires. In the dreams she brandished a sword. She pierced the heart of all who were vampire and she rode a white horse. All the vampires she had stabbed were staked and as dawn broke over the battlefield their cries filled the air as did smoke from their burning flesh. Her grandmother and mother were on either side of her. A perfect picture, Rose grinned in her sleep.

The clatter of customers in the Crimson Café brought Rose out of her slumber. Her mouth as dry as cardboard she could hardly gather enough saliva to swallow. Her stomach ached for nourishment. She slowly got up from the sofa and observed her surroundings. She lit a few candles and began to look for water or food but this was a vampires' lair. She did find some almonds and a single bottle of water in a tiny fridge at the foot of the bed where Jeremy died. Visions of Jeremy and Rebekah crept into her mind. She shook her head to clear the images. She thought about Constantine and where he could be. Should she try the tunnels again, if it were day or night, should she just go upstairs to the Café and order a grande sized caramel mocha with soy milk and extra whip and a bagel with lochs. The thought of food made her stomach grumble the nuts had done little to satiate her hunger. She had to do something. She heard a noise from deep inside the tunnels. Who's coming? Constantine, Phineas some other vampire who thinks she might make a tasty meal. Rose crawled under the bed where Jeremy had taken his last breath and she held hers. Within moments she could hear shuffling from the entrance and then actual footsteps. She closed her eyes tight. *The candles damn it!*

Chapter Twenty-Five

Rose pressed her cheek against the cold cobblestone floor, pieces of sand pinched but she had to be as still as death. Things began to fly around the room, some crashed and some shattered while tiny fragments of wood and pottery sprayed the floor. A teacup smashed against the floor in front of Rose's face followed by a growl then a huff.

Oh no.

The bed flew up and over her. Rose lay there frozen with fear she had put her head down and her arms over the back of her neck. Then with a burst of adrenaline Rose shot to her feet fist at the ready. She heard a chuckle and decided she needed to open her eyes. Thinking it was Constantine Rose began, "if you think for one –"

All air vanished from her lungs. Her eyes burned with the gathering of tears. Rose stood in shock for several long moments when suddenly her body began to shake violently. In all that trembling she bit the inside of her lip. Her hands reached out as she stumbled into the open arms of Jeff. She wrapped her arms around his neck tight as he lifted her off the floor. They stood wrapped in each other's arms for several minutes. Her trembling ceased.

Rose spoke first, "How the hell is this possible? I saw you and you were dead; did you escape, did he let you go? Oh my God, how'd you know to come here?"

Jeff let her gravity drag her body down the front of his and onto her own feet. He pushed her by the shoulders gently back away from him. Rose looked deep into his eyes and then she saw his skin although warm was without blemish, his hair curlier than usual and his eyes they were different too. As she stared the ring of red around the iris began to darken.

"No. Oh God, no, please tell me no. Not you; he didn't turn you?" She backed away several more feet shaking her head and wringing her hands.

Jeff reached for her but she flinched, he recoiled. "I'm sorry. I tried to fight it but the hunger was more than I could take. Oh, and sorry about JoAnne. It was done before I knew what I was doing."

"What?"

"I fed on your mother. I don't know how or why she was there but she just smelled so tasty, it's the only way to describe what she smelled like. I realized who she was afterward. She didn't suffer, I didn't give her a chance." Jeff hung his head in shame.

Rose began to laugh, light at first but then she roared. "You ate my mother!"

Again, Jeff began to apologize, "I'm sorry, Rose, I didn't mean to. I really didn't know it was her until it was over and she was dead. Why was she there and what is so damn funny?"

"She was Constantine's familiar. She has been with him all along. I couldn't write this shit." Rose laughed until the tears she held back trickled in a steady pink stream down her cheeks.

Jeff, without effort, appeared at her side and with his little finger he wiped the tear dangling from her chin. "Come now, it's not as bad as all that. Evidently you are changing too."

"Oh yeah, get this I'm officially a slayer. I don't think I can ever change completely because of that inherited trait." She used her right hand to demonstrate, on Jeff, a stake going into his heart but stopped just shy of touching his chest. She opened her hand placed her palm there, lovingly over his still heart.

"Really, now that is freaky. Obviously, we need to talk." Jeff placed his hand on hers and kissed her forehead ever so gently.

The two of them sat on the only piece of furniture left intact, the red settee. It was awkward at first as they stumbled for the words. But soon they fell into the same style of conversation they once knew. Rose informed him that there were other vampires on the prowl, he told her he had cleaned up the bodies and that Rebekah was in fact dead. Jeff described in detail how he had come across her and found her ancient blood to be very satisfying. Although he couldn't survive on vampire blood the occasional act of cannibalism could get one by in a pinch. Jeremy was without a doubt beyond any kind of repair. He took her body to the landfill where it will look like she was robbed, killed and dumped; another unsolved crime in a major metropolis but that the sun rose and burned whatever there was of her. She told him the tale of JoAnne and of how Dwayne took her into the caverns where she learned she was next in a long line of vampire slayers.

"So, you can kill me or at least kick my ass any time the mood strikes?" Jeff joked.

"Maybe. I am getting stronger with the little bit of Constantine's blood in me but I have no idea how to stop Constantine from turning me. I can feel his blood and when I taste blood, like I did yours, it's strange, the cravings and urges, the absolute chill I feel to my core and then there is a burst of strength, speed, vision and agility. There is a dagger at my grandmothers' house, it will stun him or paralyze him or hurt him in some way so that I can either escape or kill him, but I don't know where it is or even what it looks like. I just don't want to become an undead thing – Rose stopped she looked at Jeff who had lowered his eyes in shame. "No, I don't mean-no offense."

"Yes. you do. I was weak and ravaged another human for her blood and turned into the one thing that will keep us apart. I had no idea you'd still be alive."

"Keep us apart, why? I'm not gonna kill you. Are you gonna kill me?" Her eyes questioned him.

"Not on purpose but I'm new at this. I couldn't control myself with JoAnne, Rebekah or the twelve others."

"Twelve! Is that why you're warm, you had the blood of twelve people?"

"Yeah, but I would never hurt you even if you do smell like ambrosia." His nose sniffed the air toward her. "Your lip is bleeding."

"Oh, sorry." Rose wiped at it but missed.

"Here let me." Jeff leaned in he pulled her face up toward his. His full lips parted slightly as he slowly, gently pressed his lips to hers. They held steady for a few lingering seconds then as if on cue they began to kiss passionately and deeply. Jeff leaned his body over Rose as she relaxed under him. He wrapped one arm around her waist and lifted her off the sofa. His grip felt secure and unwavering. He lifted her up and over onto his lap. Rose wrapped both her legs around his torso and pushed into him, this made him groan. They kissed wildly as articles of clothing began to fly in different directions. Rose invited the savagery, she felt safe with Jeff. She placed her left hand between his legs, sighed long and deep. The member between his legs felt warm and hard as steel yet pliable to the touch. She nibbled his ear, whispered, "I missed you."

Insane with desire, Jeff kissed her breast and bit at her nipples until she cried out with pleasure. Hands roamed and tongues danced over various body parts. Rose lifted up onto her knees and then placed him inside her. Their bodies shuddered simultaneously. Rose began to rise and fall with controlled precision, gripping Jeff's shoulders. Soon she gave herself over to the passion rising inside her. Her thrust became hard and calculated. Jeff grabbed her hips to keep her on target. He squeezed her butt cheeks and at the crescendo of her climax he pressed her body onto his, arms around her, his face buried between her breasts. They moaned in a symphony of ecstasy. For a long time, they sat present in the moment, Jeff's cheek against her breast listening to her heart pound symphony of emotions. Rose's arms wrapped around his head her fingers stroked his hair. "It's getting cold." Rose noted as she lifted up.

Jeff closed his eyes. "It's me."

Rose looked down and touched his lips, "what?"

"You're cold because of me, I'm cooling off and fast. I'll need to feed soon. I don't want to, it's probably not safe for us to –"

She pressed two fingers to his lips, shook her head and kissed him lovingly. "I will never let you go. Do you hear me, no matter what, we will either fix this or live with it but I refuse to give you up."

Rose lifted off him and pulled on her jeans.

"I'll be back as soon as I can. Wait here?" Jeff asked with a pleading look in his eyes. He had his clothes on in seconds and stood before her with bated breath.

"I'll be here. But I don't know when Constantine will be back. Please, hurry."

They kissed in the safety of loving arms. And, he was gone.

Rose pulled her sweatshirt over her head when she felt the breeze. She spun in a circle but saw no one.

"Well, that'll teach you."

"Who's there?" She, demanded. "I know you're here damn it, show yourself, coward!"

"Give your heart to a man who turns vamp and he can't wait to go feed."

In an instant Rose found herself on the floor. A weight on her chest prevented a full breath, one she desperately needed. Out of the haze came the face of Phineas. White hair, white skin and black eyes with a touch of red in the iris, his lips parted as if speaking to her but her ears still rang from contact with the floor.

"Well?" He tilted his head to one side.

"Well, what? I can't breathe." Rose groaned out the words.

"Oh, sorry, Mon Cheri." He lifted a tiny bit and Rose took the opportunity to pull herself out from under him. She stood before she had time to think about what she was going to do. He applauded and chuckled.

"Brava." The vampire clapped his hands in a sarcastic flimsy manner. "You are gaining instincts more quickly than I would have guessed possible. And you've not even fully changed. I reckon your slayer side is competing with your vampire side. Ooh, I wonder who shall win." The slight Cajun-French accent didn't match the vampire's appearance but it was welcome to hear something other than Constantine's old-world lingo.

"Yeah, and just you remember that." Rose retorted with some half-baked courage.

"Ha! I love it." Phineas spun in a circle. "We are goin' to be fast friends, you and I."

"I don't think so. You're vampire, I'm slayer. We aren't meant to be friends." Rose took a step backwards.

"Oh, like you and Romeo?"

"You saw that?" Rose looked away and blushed.

"I heard you way before I subjected my poor eyes to the glory of your sex. I waited politely till it was over. I have a proposition for you." He smiled devilishly.

"Reaaa-lly?" Sarcasm soaked all three syllables of the word.

"Don't be coy, sha. I know you want Constantine off your back, so to speak. So do I."

"Why? I thought vamps stuck together." Rose put her hands together and squeezed.

"No. By nature we are loners. You know this, it's what attracted you to our kind. The few covens here and there are mostly made up of one vampire who likes to have minions and a bunch of newbies who don't know which end of a person to bite. We are fiercely protective of territory, like my home Lake Charles. A beautiful paradise thick with culture, swamps and juicy people with spice." He lifted one eyebrow to get his point across. "I was hunted from my home by none other than your ancestor Violette, when she was about your age. I came here looking to get vengeance on her but found you know who and I have been fighting for people juice ever since. I see his attraction to you and he is so enthralled he can't see your aura of slayer." He waved his hands in a womanly figure in the air.

"Wait," Rose said sharp with her hand in a stop position, "I have a slayer aura?"

"Of course, you do. Vampires see in many dimensions. An aura is just the electrical impulse your body puts out and let me tell you Mon Cheri, yours impresses. Of course, your potential maker can't see it. And, that sha, gives me and you an advantage."

"How so?" Rose relaxed her stance and looked inquisitively at the strange albino-Cajun vampire.

"Looks like you're beginning to get my thought process." He took a step to one side, moving slowly so as not to alert Rose into some knee jerk reaction that could cause her injury.

He bowed and then sat on the settee he patted the seat next to him, "Still warm."

Phineas winked.

"Now, whatever should we do about our mutual enemy?" He crossed his legs and placed both hands on top of his knee twisted his foot back and forth at the ankle.

"Well, I guess that depends on the number of vampire secrets you're willing to share." Rose sat on the settee next to Phineas. He flashed his pearly white fangs and leaned in close.

"It all began when Louisiana seceded from the Union."

"You mean the Civil War, 125 plus years ago?"

"Yes. Well, almost. Towards the end of the war."

"Constantine led me to believe he was much older than that."

"Ha! That compulsively lying tick! He was turned in the same mud hole I was, the battlefield. He may talk fancy but that's because he was a rich, spoiled, highly educated southerner who lived up North and thought his shit didn't stink. To tell you the truth, baby girl, he was just as bad alive as he is undead. I had been fighting, I mean chewing and clawing my way with my regiment but that fateful night I was killed by a Union soldier's bayonet. I lay there bleeding from the gaping wound in my belly, dying slowly as others around me cried out in pain and then silently succumbed. I awaited my turn and then the moment just before my death I watched in utter shock as a dozen or more slave vampires snuck onto the still burning battlefield. I heard screams and suckles. All of a sudden there was a face before me. He had to be the biggest black man I'd ever seen. Well, he tells me that I was the whitest white person he'd ever seen, as I'm albino, and he was gonna give me the gift of never dying. I awoke to what you see before you now. I survived the way others had by taking the dying on the battlefield. It was easy pickins until I came across a dying Union soldier named Samuel James Paxton in the woods of Tennessee. The battle of Franklin to be exact, November 30 1864."

Rose shifted, cocked her head to one side, "Wait. Who is that?"

Phineas smiled, "He calls himself Constantine."

"Are you joking? Constantine is really a Samuel! He's been lying to me!"

"Cheri, vampires will do anything for a little juice. They will make you think they love you. They will give you great sexual pleasure and even promise you the moon. But my boy Samuel is a full-fledged narcissistic, pathological liar. Once he got the taste of blood, he went crazy on those Confederate soldiers, living and dying. Rumor is he took out a general or two. I moved back to New Orleans after the war to heal my own wounds."

"Who turned him?"

"A slave. A young girl about 14, just turned and starving, she paid with her life though. She fed off Samuel, er, Constantine and just as she was about to take that last drop he bit back. He retrieved all of his blood and hers. That is how he turned. It was not pretty. Did he tell you the story about how he captured a vamp so he could turn himself?"

"Yep. That's the story I got."

"Tsk-tsk, Mon Cheri. It is the way of Samuel, the liar. Now, let's get busy on how we can stop him before he screws things up for all of us. Ever hear of a vampire killing dagger?"

Chapter Twenty-Six

Rose sat quietly on the settee and waited. She reflected on how drastically her life had changed. One day a lonely author and the next day a half-vampire-half-slayer plotting with an albino vampire for the demise of a lying, pretentious vampire. Except now, not so lonely, not as long as she had Jeff and that could be a very long time.

"Lord, not sure if you're still there or even listening but if you are I need help. This may sound odd but I figure you have some experience with these sorts of things. I have to take on a vampire who wants nothing more than to make me one. I don't know that I can do this." Rose rung her hands together to warm them then shook out her fingers. "I don't want to bargain with you. I probably don't have a lot of credit to my side but if you could see your way to lending me a hand, I'd really appreciate it and I'd try to do better as far as the lord name in vain stuff. I can't promise much more than that but I could use the help."

Her voice quieted and her inner voice started in on her.

You're an idiot if you think you can defeat a vampire. You write books in the safety of your darkened room. What do you really know about a living breathing, ok, subjective. Let's see, they need blood, sunlight is the ultimate death, silver burns them, holy objects have little effect on them. Wait? That one came from Constantine, he lies. And, recently you learned that a certain thorned rose bush can render a vampire paralyzed as well as tear their skin to shreds. Last but not least there is a dagger, blessed by a Pope with holy water that can either kill or maim a vampire. All I have to do is entice him with blood, find the silver dagger, stab him, toss him into the thorn bushes and then wait for the sun to do its' job. Great plan, as long as everyone does their part. Oh, and a miracle from God.

Rose laughed out loud. *Oh, my God! What are you thinking? It'll never work.*

"What is so amusing?" The voice echoed but without doubt belonged to Constantine.

Rose yelled toward the opening of the tunnel, "Lucy, I'm home!"

Next to her ear she felt the temperature change and knew he was within inches of her. Her body tensed and an icy shiver ran down to her tailbone. Rose resisted the urge to run.

"Not funny." Constantine whispered in her ear. Then paced around her. He lifted his nose in the air several times. "You were not alone, now were you? I smell others on you."

"Really, you leave me alone here for God knows how long without food, water, wine or a shower. I haven't had any decent facilities since, oh I can't remember. Of course, I probably smell like underground Atlanta. Get me the hell out of here!"

"As you wish." Constantine wrapped his arms around Rose's waist lifted and ran. They quickly came to an intersection in the tunnels. Above them a trap door with roots growing all around it. Constantine bulleted into the dilapidated wood. It succumbed, raining down shards into the tunnel at Rose's' feet. Constantine grabbed her wrist and pulled her up into the night air. Looking back, she could see they had just escaped from an abandoned shaft or well. Crickets sang their songs and the cicada chimed in harmoniously. Rose took in a deep breath and looked skyward. The stars twinkled bright as was their duty. The air hung heavy with smell of roses and azaleas.

Chapter Twenty-Seven

She stood in front of the house on Gordon Place where she lost her entire family to violence and the whims of a vampire.

Her stomach knotted and acid churned in her esophagus. What is he going to do now? Rose pondered, as she bit her lip, a nervous habit she thought she'd broken.

Constantine dusted himself off. His standard uniform, black slacks, black silk collarless pull-over and a black silken jacket. "I came here before you, while you rested at the Café, so I could make things ready. It felt lonely to have slept here without you."

"Ready for what?"

"Your complete and total surrender and eventual change. I will have my way. We can do this easily without a lot of screaming and resistance but I am not completely against a little fight. I like it rough from time to time. Shall we." Constantine extended his arm to allow Rose to go before him toward the front of the house.

A dog barked, Constantine growled and the dog went silent. "You go in first, I will be along in a moment." He gave Rose a push on her lower back that made her stumble forward several steps.

"Okay, I'll just go in now." She looked back Constantine was gone again.

"Hey!" A half-muffled yell came from the bushes around the front porch. Rose leaned in and jumped with a start as Dwayne popped up and out of the bushes. He gave her an enthusiastic two thumbs up and ran next door to his own house.

He really thinks I can kill this vamp.

Rose took a deep breath and walked the few passes to the steps of the porch. They were painted a fiery red so with the white trim they really stood out. The white columns and beige trim around the house gave a nod to the strength of Southern architecture. Rose trembled as her fingers grabbed the doorknob and turned, it surrendered easily. Inside, the room felt lived in and happy. The furniture even felt more inviting than before when she was here with the Sheriff. The warm glow from the lit fireplace reminded her of the way she felt in the presence of her mothers' spirit, loved.

She stepped into the living room, the door snapped shut behind her, the fire flickered and went out.

An icy chill whipped past her cheek lifting a lock of her hair and twirling it. "I know I should not tease but you are so delectable. To smell your fear is truly tantalizing. As a child you had no fear of me. I found that fascinating. I suppose it is adults who create fear among children. But that is a topic for later discussion. We will have eternity to ponder what ever our hearts desire."

Constantine let go a chilling breathe on the nape of her neck. She refused to move, to respond. He wrapped his arms around her waist from behind and lifted her to his mouth. She felt the cold flesh of his tongue on her ear and then on her cheek. She shivered.

"Do you mind if I take a shower and use the restroom before we get started? You know, my human business. Besides I don't think I can face eternity without getting cleaned up first."

Constantine huffed, "If you must. Make it quick, we do not have all night. I am desirous of your sweetness in my arms for eternity. Go." He turned her by her shoulders towards the hallway.

The shower was decadent; when Rose finished, she pulled back the curtain to find a set of clothes, jeans and a blousy white top. Without thinking about the origin of them Rose dried off and dressed. *How could I not remember this place?* She used a comb from the medicine cabinet to detangle her long hair. In the mirror she examined her image. She looked the same, maybe tired but nearly flawless skin in a slightly olive tone. Her eyes a tad puffy but overall she wasn't half the worse for the wear. She opened the door to Constantine.

He put a hand on either side of the door jam and leaned in to whisper, "I will do for you what no one else had the power to. I will give you back all of the memories I have kept from you."

"You actually did that?"

"I veiled them; I can release them." He took Rose in his arms and danced her back into the living room where the fired burned brightly again. He began to rock side to side, gently at first then he turned and spun in a circle faster and faster till Rose felt she would vomit. The spinning room at one glance was a blur but began to develop into distorted images and then with a jolt came total clarity.

"Look Rose, look at your childhood." Constantine turned so she could see the rest of the room before them.

Rose lifted her head, opened her eyes to see the room had completed its' transformation. A small lamp between the sofa and armchair the only light source gave off a yellow glow. A shout came from somewhere in the back of the house, a man's voice, angry. The windows rattled with the stomping footsteps running down the hall. A whimper, Rose turned to see a little girl hiding in the corner by the front window hunkered down behind the armchair. The man appeared in the living room with a large saber. It glistened in the dim light. Sweat dripped from the man's nose. His hands trembled, his eyes wide and his face red. He stood still, listened, dressed in unbuckled camouflage pants with untied boots and no shirt.

Rose turned her eyes back to the little girl, "Sssh he'll hear you!"

"They cannot hear you." Constantine hissed. "It has already happened there is nothing you can do but watch."

"That's me, isn't it?"

"Yes. It is my dear and that is your father. Keep watching it will get better. Oh, so much better."

The man with the saber knelt down on his knees, "I know you're here.

You can't hide. I won't let you kill us in our sleep like your Viet-kong sisters did to my men in Da Nang. Come on out, it's okay."

The little girl whimpered grabbed her mouth with both hands and shook her head violently. The man lunged over the chair and in seconds he had her. She dangled from his right arm as he pulled the flat of the blade gingerly across her forehead. "Gottcha, you commie bitch! Who you gonna kill now, huh!"

The girl kicked in rapid succession at the man but he was oblivious to the blows.

"Let her alone, George." Grannie aimed a gun directly at the man. "I said put her down or I'll blow your head clean off, and you know I can do it."

"She's gonna kill us in our sleep? I can't put her down. Can't you see the yellow in her eyes?"

"Charles, you're not in Nam. You're at home and that little girl is Rose, your baby girl. Put her down now! I - ain't - gonna – tell – you - again."

A scream ignited the chain of events that followed. The man jumped onto the chair and held the girl by one arm and raised the saber high above his head. Rose watched frozen as the blast from the gun lit the entire room and filled it with smoke simultaneously. Everything slowed to a millisecond.

"I thought you would really want to see the detail in the next few moments so I have slowed it for you." Constantine tightened his grip around Roses waist. She let out the breath she'd forgotten about.

The bullet charged steady at the man's chest hitting him with fatal accuracy. His body recoiled with tremendous violence, the knife already in motion followed alongside the trail of the bullet to its' target, Grannie. The man's chest exploded into tiny shreds of flesh, meat and bones, the little girl landed against the front door and fell into a heap. Grannie stood frozen momentarily, dropped the gun, pulled at the knife buried deep inside her throat. Unable to budge it she fell to her knees. Her eyes filled with disbelieving tears as she looked over at Rose. Her lips gathered in a painful grimace she reached out her hand to Rose then relaxed into death as she fell backwards. Another scream brought the room out of slow motion. The screaming woman stepped over Grannie and grabbed the little girl. She stepped around the chair containing the mangled body of Rose's father. The little girl, covered in blood, made no sound. The woman, Rose's mother Elizabeth, picked up and cradled the little girl and sat on the sofa with her. She rocked back and forth with the little girl wrapped tightly in her arms. She sang the same lullaby as the one she sang at the asylum. Rose could no longer contain the pain; her head throbbed her eyes burned her head fell forward against Constantine's icy chest. Rose sobbed.

"It is not yet done. This is the best part." Constantine pulled at Rose's hair until she looked up at the next scene.

Another Constantine appeared from the back of the house, the Constantine from that time. He glided toward the little girl and her mother.

The mother screamed, "No!" She placed Rose on the sofa then stood and ran to the fireplace mantle. She grabbed and tore at a book, a bible.

Rose turned a little in Constantine's arms to see better, it was the family bible her mother was so desperate to grab. *Why the Bible?*

Constantine slapped the mother with the back of his hand she flew to the other side of the room bouncing off the door and onto the floor next to Grannie. The Elizabeth scrambled for the book again this time on her hands and knees while the little girl sat motionless.

"You cannot kill me with your pathetic religious memorabilia." He laughed as he kicked the mother to the sofa. She reached for the little girl and Constantine kicked her again. He picked up the little girl in almost the exact same fashion he now held Rose. The mother snorted a painful ragged breath as Constantine stepped on the bible and twisted it under his foot. Rose noticed a glimmer from the book. A blade. Her mother, so desperate and feeble in her attempt, cried out. Rose remembered that her grandmother had shown her the dagger on several occasions and promised that one day it would belong to Rose and she would know exactly how to use it to destroy vampires. The relic was indeed very special a once glorious Pope had blessed the relic personally. It was always kept safe and within reach in the center pages of the family bible.

Constantine laughed simultaneously with the past Constantine, "I never get tired of doing that."

The mother lunged at Constantine again but he grabbed her by the throat with one hand and lifted her several feet off the floor. "I will let you live because you will serve a great purpose."

With his other hand he lifted the young Rose from the floor and placed the her on the sofa. He held tight to the mother while he drank from Rose's father. When he had finished, he dragged the body off the chair and tossed it on top of the dead grandmother. Then he fed on Rose's mother. When Constantine finished with her, he shoved her shell of a body back on the sofa. Her eyes rolled up and then went blank, her catatonia secure. Flashing red and blue lights filled the blood-splattered room and then everything flashed to present.

Rose wiped at the tears on her face the flood of memories had finally taken their place in her mind and in her heart. Her Grannie showing her the cavern, the relics and detailing the family heritage that would soon be handed down to Rose. Rose's mother refused the gifts and focused all her love, and teaching on Rose.

"Damn you to hell!" She grabbed at his face with her nails. Constantine brushed her hands away.

"Probably, but I knew you would love it. I wanted you to see it all and understand what a great gift you are about to receive. I allowed you to live so you could have eternity with me. Your grandmother was the one I could have feared, after all, it was she who believed your wild stories of the devil in the garden. She had a strong soul and would have fought much harder. Thankfully your war-crazed father took care of her, an amazing twist of fate. And, feeding from them both was a coup d'état. We are, as one might say, blood relation."

He released her. Rose stepped away from him. She felt a new resolve take hold. She now knew who she was and what she had been raised to be and what she needed to do in order to avenge her families' death and save to her own life.

She turned toward the darkened fireplace and made her way toward it as she spoke. "I can't believe you did that to my family. If all you wanted was me, why didn't you just finish me then and there in the Magnolia tree? Why waste so much time, money and effort on me?"

"Nothing I have done is a waste, least of all with you. I never wanted a companion until I tasted your blood. I wanted you, as an adult, with your fearlessness intact and your richness of spirit. I have never felt as alive as I did with your blood coursing through my body. I have spared no expense to keep you perfect. Your family, a mere casualty, they were destined to destroy themselves, I happened upon this scene. Except for your mother, she gave me great leverage. I was brilliant for keeping her alive as long as I did."

While he elaborated on his accomplishments Rose looked around for the bible and spied it on the floor next to the liquor cabinet. She turned, a wisp of air broke across her face, Constantine stood next to her. Her hand trembled, "I need a drink. It will steady my nerves."

He laughed. "Please, by all means, partake of your last dose of human courage. After tonight you will never need anything but blood." He walked behind her and with one hand lifted her hair away from the left side of her neck. He licked her then turned toward the fireplace. She shivered and poured the amber liquid into the snifter. She lifted the bible from the floor with one hand and held it close to her chest, the dagger now hidden inside the sleeve of her shirt.

Constantine chuckled, "I have been under the impression you did not subscribe to such beliefs?"

"I don't. It's just my mother did and that makes it dear to me. It gives me strength and a reason to be thankful you didn't kill me or her that night." She drank the liquor in one gulp and slammed the glass down.

Constantine grabbed the book and hurled it across the room.

"You have had enough courage for one night, I am no longer patient. I allowed you to live, for me."

He grabbed Rose up and cradled her in his arms. He carried her down the long hall past the family portraits, through the back door and across the porch. He dropped her to her feet next to the Magnolia. Lifting the deep green branches of the tree, he shoved her into the darkened space.

"I like the musty smell." He lifted his nose high into the air and drew in deeply.

Rose stood still not sure what was to happen next just that she needed to find the dagger. But Constantine knew what he wanted. He walked around her in a tight circle sniffed her, touched her. His body felt colder than it ever had felt before and he looked more pale than usual. In a sudden swoosh a jolt to her stomach took her breath away. As her body slammed into the trunk of the Magnolia tree, she felt the dagger slip from her sleeve. Her legs, like gelatin, could not hold her up. Before she hit the ground, she felt her body lifted again and then tossed back into the air. Her back hit flat on the ground. Her head bounced twice leaving a ringing sound in her ears and a touch of nausea in her throat. Her vision came and went. Constantine pounced on top of her. His face almost touching hers he inhaled deep and exhaled with a moan.

"When you have become like me, we will play together more easily. I do not wish to hurt you. Bruised blood is distasteful. Once I have drained you and filled you with my precious blood, we will escape the coming sunrise and go to ground together to seal our union."

Rose watched intently as Constantine's eyes rolled back into their sockets turning them a coal black like a shark about to frenzy feed. His extended fangs glistened.

The sun's coming!

His body became rigid. He yanked her head to the right and grabbed her neck forcing her vein to bulge. He bit hard. First, she heard the soft pop then she felt the piercing of her jugular and the tug against her heart as he began to suck. Each long drag produced a dizzy sensation and a stabbing pain that radiated throughout her entire body.

Dear god, please let me find the dagger!

She dug the fingernails of her left hand deep into the flesh of her palm. She had to hold on for just a few more seconds. Her right hand groped until it found the tip of hilt. She scratch at the ground with her fingertips and found the handle. Rose could feel the blade surrender to her as it lifted from the dirt. The fear she'd felt her entire life dissipated. In its place was the strength of family, heritage and her desire to live. The other hand she brought up and rubbed along Constantine's back between his shoulder blades. He moaned long and heavy. Rose could feel his full weight on her and his full sex. It began to throb against her as he filled himself with her warm life giving blood.

Typical man.

Stars danced in front of her eyes so she closed them tight. She settled on the spot just between two vertebrae and alongside the spine. Rose wrapped both arms around him, he responded, she thrust the blade deep into her molester. His mouth opened wide but released no sound. She felt blood drip onto her neck and face. She opened her eyes to see his face contorted in pain and disbelief. She plunged the knife deeper, to the hilt. Unable to speak or move Constantine stared at Rose. It made her smile to see the unmitigated horror on his blood-stained face. She pulled her body up toward his and whispered in his ear, "Rose's gone a hunting . . ."

Quick as a vampire, she dug her heels into the dirt to shuffle her body out from under Constantine. She scrambled to steady herself and stood, her head reeled from the lack of blood. Her left knee buckled then the right. Her out-stretched hand caught the ground before her. She looked up to see Constantine writhing as he tried to free the blade lodged firmly in his back. The flesh around the silver blade sizzled loud enough for Rose to know she had found the sweet spot. Constantine could not reach the blade to take it out. The blade made of silver and just long enough to tap into the vile lifeless heart of a monster, scorched him from the inside out. Streams of blood from every orifice made its way down to his stomach and soaked his silk shirt. Rose tried to stand again only to tumble backwards landing outside the tree. She took a deep breath and composed her thoughts. On the horizon, the sun, a blood orange glow with a promise to rise; the first rays would burst forth soon. *Constantine has to be outside the Magnolia and near enough to the grove of wild roses if I'm gonna have a chance.*

She willed her body to stand.

"Constantine! Did you think I wouldn't fight?" She touched the wounds on her neck no blood flowed. Rose could already feel her body begin to heal.

A growl crawled from the darkness, "I counted on it."

Constantine stepped out of the safety of the limbs. His eyes pulsed with anger as the vein in the middle of his forehead throbbed creating a blue streak against his porcelain skin. He took on a more monstrous appearance with each staggered step. Beads of blood sweat dotted his face.

"I should have killed you, sucked you dry of that intractable soul you possess. You will not complete your lame attempt. I will heal and you will turn. I will have you." He lurched, coughed, blood sprayed from his lips. Each time he reached for the knife he howled in pain. Unable to remove it, he looked upward and howled in agony.

"YOU DO NOT OWN ME, STEPHEN!" Rose cried with a deadly sarcasm.

Constantine charged; his arms reached out for her as he fell into air, Rose spun to her right at the last possible second. Constantine grasped a fist full of her hair. Rose twisted back around so that she faced Constantine. She kicked him solidly in the stomach. With her new found strength Rose was able to launch him several feet into the air. He flailed against gravity but landed prostrate atop the wild thorn roses. The steely thorns ripped into his translucent flesh. Blood squirted in all directions. The thorns trapped him in their claw like grip. Each struggled motion dug the thorns deeper into his flesh. Blood began to flow in steady streams. As each drop of blood met the scorching sunlight it turned to ash and floated on the gentle morning breeze. Constantine's flesh suddenly and violently burst into a pyre of blue, red and orange. He bellowed and screamed obscenities as Rose had never heard and in a multitude of languages. His flesh melted and dripped to the dirt. Rose studied the process as his body contorted violently and his flesh seared to the bone. The bone began to char and flake away to ash. Each fleck sparkled as it lifted into the sky on the wings of the breeze to flitter and flutter until so utterly destroyed they simply failed to exist.

Exhaustion overcame Rose. She collapsed onto the top step of the upper terrace as the rising sun cooked what was left of Constantine 'the Vampire'. She listened intently to every shriek and guttural moan. She waited patiently until the last ash of his existence had fluttered away on the wind before she stood with her arms out stretched, her face aimed full on into the warming rays of the sun, not knowing if she would burn or be cured. Her skin tightened and tingled then turned pale amber, but she did not burn. Constantine existed no more, not in flesh and not in her.

Rose sat on the swing that she now remembered she had played on as a child and gently pushed off with one foot to engage the back-and-forth motion. *What now? I am free of Constantine but what does that mean for my books? And, what do I do about the other vamp, kill him too. I need to get the dagger it actually gave me the strength I needed to fight back. Do I really want to be a slayer? Do I hunt them or will they find me. This will make for good reading.*

After several minutes Rose paused, "Damn, I need to rewrite that last chapter."

Chapter Twenty-Eight

Whispers snaked along the line of anxious fans. One woman asked, "What do you think she'll look like?"

Another answered, "I heard she got burned pretty bad but she went to some place in Belgium and got new skin."

A man bellowed, "Impossible, the whole thing was just a publicity stunt. I'll bet her agent is still alive too, hidden away somewhere."

In the front of the line an elderly woman barked, "And, you call yourselves fans. Just be thankful she survived that explosion! She may never've been able to write again, then where would you be, re-reading the same books over and over. I for one could care less how she looks as long as she's willing to write. This new book is amazing, I think she got even better."

A hush fell soft like a velvet blanket lain over a parakeet's gilded cage. Everyone aimed eyes towards the woman from behind the counter of the Daily Grind coffee house. The little establishment could not contain the number of people who waited for an autograph, a photo or even a glimpse of the author.

Rose felt a gurgle of excitement bubble into her throat. *People, I need people.*

She made her way to the beautiful high back floral print armchair behind a delicate antique table at the beginning of a very long line of adoring fans. The silence deafened, a waiter pulled out the chair and Rose scooted her bottom onto the firm cushion. "Thank you."

She smiled at the young man who brought back longing memories of

Jeremy. A pang of sadness touched her heart and she looked up at the adoring faces of her fans. "Good evening, who's first?"

And, with that an excitement washed over the crowd. The noise level quickly rose with chatter about the book.

An hour into the signing a young woman shyly approached, "This is the most romantic story I've ever read. I want to be a writer one day and you are my hero. Where do you get this stuff? I mean, "My Everyday Life as a Vampire's Wife", c'mon. That is some cool stuff."

"Well, it's all in here." Rose taps her temple with her index finger. "But, the really good stuff is in here." And, she pointed to her heart. "Write to please your heart and your words will find their intended target. After all that is why we write is it not, to please some deep-rooted need growing within ourselves. Fill that need with your words and someone will read them. Good luck and if you need any help with your writing call me." She handed the signed book back to the young lady.

As the fan walked away, she examined the page and giggled when she saw a phone number and the words, *call me anytime.*

Just then a waitress walked up with a glass of ice tea and a note. Rose thanked her and sipped the sweet nectar. She asked the person in line to wait just a moment and opened the sealed envelope. Inside, a note neatly penned read:

> *My dearest,*
> *I miss you, can't wait to hold you in my arms.*
> *See you soon.*
>
> > *Your adoring husband,*
> > *Jeff*

Rose pulled the note to her chest and sighed deeply. *I love you too.*

"Where was I?" Rose grabbed a book from the stack to her left to autograph. Her right hand discreetly caressed her abdomen, she felt the flutter of movement from the precious life growing inside her. She smiled sweetly knowing her one true love would be there for her, always and forever.

Just outside the coffee house a pair of blood rimmed eyes twitched.

About the Author

Marie Valden is by nature a poet. Since the day her grandmother gave her a Big Chief notebook and a pencil she has been writing. She has written content, short stories, poetry, non-fiction, fiction, and no matter what else she has done in her life writing is the constant that fills her cup and allows her to wander freely among the characters she sets loose.

She lives in Dallas, Texas with her chihuahua Chloe and spends as much time as she can with her daughters and granddaughters.

www.ingramcontent.com/pod-product-compliance
Lightning Source LLC
Chambersburg PA
CBHW061102100726
47911CB00012B/352